'About the job.' If you could legitimately call pretending to be engaged to a Greek millionaire a job. **'Were you serious?'**

His expression sharpened. 'You'll do it?'

'Don't look smug just yet,' she warned him quickly.

Mathieu watched her hair blow in the wind and struggled to control a sudden overwhelming compulsion to mesh his fingers into the silky strands...then he could draw her face up to his and— He sucked in a deep breath.

'But you're thinking about it...?' he prompted, while his own thoughts stayed stubbornly fixated on the soft, lush outline of her lips.

And Mathieu knew the fun was about to begin...

D0674516

Kim Lawrence lives on a farm in rural Anglesey. She runs two miles daily, and finds this an excellent opportunity to unwind and seek inspiration for her writing! It also helps her keep up with her husband, two active sons, and the various stray animals which have adopted them. Always a fanatical consumer of fiction, she is now equally enthusiastic about writing. She loves a happy ending!

**Kim's fast-paced, exciting stories,
packed full of sizzling attraction and sexy men,
will whisk you away!**

THE DEMETRIOS BRIDAL BARGAIN

BY
KIM LAWRENCE

MILLS & BOON
Pure reading pleasure

DID YOU PURCHASE THIS BOOK WITHOUT A COVER?

If you did, you should be aware it is **stolen property** as it was reported
unsold and destroyed by a retailer. Neither the author nor the publisher
has received any payment for this book.

All the characters in this book have no existence outside the imagination
of the author, and have no relation whatsoever to anyone bearing the
same name or names. They are not even distantly inspired by any
individual known or unknown to the author, and all the incidents are
pure invention.

All Rights Reserved including the right of reproduction in whole or
in part in any form. This edition is published by arrangement with
Harlequin Enterprises II BV/S.à.r.l. The text of this publication or
any part thereof may not be reproduced or transmitted in any form
or by any means, electronic or mechanical, including photocopying,
recording, storage in an information retrieval system, or otherwise,
without the written permission of the publisher.

This book is sold subject to the condition that it shall not, by way of
trade or otherwise, be lent, resold, hired out or otherwise circulated
without the prior consent of the publisher in any form of binding or
cover other than that in which it is published and without a similar
condition including this condition being imposed on the subsequent
purchaser.

® and TM are trademarks owned and used by the trademark owner
and/or its licensee. Trademarks marked with ® are registered with the
United Kingdom Patent Office and/or the Office for Harmonisation in
the Internal Market and in other countries.

First published in Great Britain 2007
Harlequin Mills & Boon Limited,
Eton House, 18-24 Paradise Road, Richmond, Surrey TW9 1SR

© Kim Lawrence 2007

ISBN: 978 0 263 85374 2

Set in Times Roman 10 on 12¼ pt
01-1207-53437

Printed and bound in Spain
by Litografia Rosés, S.A., Barcelona

THE DEMETRIOS
BRIDAL BARGAIN

CHAPTER ONE

ANDREOS DEMETRIOS, his erect posture making no concession to the whirling blades of the helicopter from which he had just alighted, looked around, his piercing dark glance moving pointedly over and past his reception committee—a younger man standing beside the helicopter pad.

It was a deliberate snub, but nothing in the waiting man's expression suggested that he was affronted by the action. His only response at all was the faintest of sardonic smiles as the older man pointedly turned his back to him.

People did not, as a rule, overlook Mathieu Demetrios. It wasn't just his height—Mathieu topped six four—or his face, though more column inches than he cared to recall had been devoted to his classical profile, which many writers claimed, with what Mathieu considered a lack of originality, could have graced a Greek coin. No, what Mathieu Demetrios had was far less quantifiable; he had that rare indefinable quality—he had presence.

When Mathieu spoke people listened. When he walked into a room heads turned, people watched him—people, that is, who weren't his father. The same father who was at that moment delivering a string of terse rapid instructions to the bespectacled man who had just disembarked with him from the helicopter.

Mathieu's patrician features gave no hint of his feelings as, silver eyes narrowing, he silently observed the interchange. He held himself with natural grace, his body language relaxed as an updraft from the helicopter blades plastered his thin shirt against his body revealing the clearly defined musculature of his powerful shoulders and chest, the same squall tugging at his dark hair.

The man nodding respectfully as he listened to Andreos Demetrios was the only one of the trio who was made visibly uncomfortable by the tension and simmering hostility vibrating in the disturbed air.

Keeping one wary eye on his employer, he risked the Greek financier's wrath by sending the younger man a tentative smile of sympathy before he hurried past him. It was hard to tell whether the gesture was either noticed or appreciated. Unlike his father, Mathieu Gauthier, or Demetrios as they must learn to call him, kept his cards pretty close to his chest and he definitely was not prone to the uncontrolled outbursts of emotion for which Andreos was famed.

If Mathieu Demetrios had been a different sort of man, the sort who looked as if he would appreciate well-meaning advice, he might have taken the younger man to one side and explained that the older man's mood changes, though abrupt, could sometimes be diverted if you learnt to read the danger signs.

Even simply showing a little reaction to his father's outbursts, excepting Mathieu's usual cynical amusement or boredom, would help.

Opinion amongst employees who had to witness the conflict firsthand was split into two camps when it came to the subject of the uneasy relationship between Andreos and his heir apparent. Personally, his logical accountant's brain could not allow him to believe that anyone would deliberately go out of his way to provoke Andreos Demetrios. No, he joined those who said it was a matter of perception, and someone who had hurled a formula-one car at speed around a track for a living as Mathieu Gauthier had could not be expected to perceive danger the same way normal mortals did.

It was only after the third man had left that the Greek financier faced his son. Andreos had read and reread the comprehensive report he had requested during the flight from the mainland searching for errors.

If there had been flaws in the report he would have found them; there were none. It was clear, concise and drew some unexpected but challenging conclusions, which only seemed obvious once they had been pointed out.

Challenging about summed up his eldest son. A nerve jerked in Andreos's heavy jaw as his eyes, dark and contemptuous, swept upwards from the feet of the younger man to his face.

Only once in all their years of marriage had Andreos ever broken his vows of fidelity to the wife he adored; it was a moment he had regretted and been ashamed of ever since.

But to have the physical proof of that infidelity appear in the form of a sullen, self-contained male adolescent who did not further endear himself to his reluctant father by outperforming his legitimate half-brother in every way both intellectual and athletic had been a nightmare situation.

Ironically it had been his wronged wife, Mia, not Andreos, who had been able to welcome the motherless boy into their home with genuine warmth.

The noise of the helicopter engine faded at the same moment the men's eyes locked—smouldering brown with cool grey.

They stayed that way for a long time.

The older man was the first to lower his gaze. A dull angry colour dusted his cheeks and heavy jaw and he addressed his son. He did not waste time on preliminaries.

'You will cancel your little trip to...' a spasm of irritation crossed Andreos's heavy swarthy features as he trawled his memory '…wherever it was you were going.'

There was no trace of warmth or affection in his curt demand, but Mathieu did not expect it. His father had never made any pretence of affection, but before Alex's death Andreos had not been as overtly hostile as he was now. But then before Alex's death twelve months had been able to go by without father and his elder son meeting.

But Alex's death had changed that.

It had, Mathieu reflected bleakly, changed a lot of things.

'Scotland.'

'Well, you can change your plans.'

It was not a suggestion. But then the head of Demetrios Enterprises, a global giant that had major interests in amongst other things IT and telecommunications—things had moved on since the days the family were merely Greek shipping million-aires—did not make suggestions.

Andreos Demetrios spoke and people jumped.

The recipient of this peremptory decree wasn't showing any signs of jumping. Mathieu wasn't doing anything; in fact he achieved a level of stillness that very few people ever managed. His eyes narrowed but it was impossible to tell what emotion lay concealed beneath the mirrored silver surface and his enigmatic expression was equally uninformative.

Not that Andreos in his turn seemed interested in his son's response. After issuing his pronouncement the older man began to walk briskly up the winding white marble path that led to a massive villa complex that was built into the pink rock above the sparkling turquoise waters of the Aegean.

Andreos had reached the edge of the lush landscaped grounds that surrounded the villa when Mathieu caught up with him.

'I am going to Scotland to stay with a friend; the plan is not flexible.'

The trip was only partly pleasure; Jamie had asked for his help. The banks were making unhappy noises and the fate of the highland estate his friend had inherited from his father the previous year hung in the balance.

Unless I come up with one hell of a business plan they won't extend the loans, Mathieu. That means I won't just be the MacGregor who couldn't hack it as formula-one driver, I'll be the MacGregor who lost the estate that has been in the family for five hundred years.

The older man swung back, his expression antagonistic. 'Were going. Sacha and her mother are arriving tomorrow.'

Mathieu repressed a sigh, reflecting that he really ought to have anticipated this.

'A fact you neglected to mention when you summoned me.'

The older man gave a thin-lipped smile. 'It would be an insult to them if you are not here. There have been links between the Constantine family and ours for generations. My father and—'

'And,' Mathieu inserted, interrupting the history lesson, 'there is no son in this generation to inherit and you hate the idea of the Constantine fortune slipping through your grubby fingers.'

A flash of anger darkened the older man's heavy features. 'And I suppose you would turn your nose up at it?' he grunted.

'I wouldn't be prepared to marry a girl of nineteen to get it.' A girl who had coincidentally been engaged to his younger brother. When he had first heard of the engagement, Mathieu had been inclined to view it with cynicism.

Not so much a marriage as a merger.

But Mathieu's view had changed once he had seen the two youngsters together. They had been very obviously in love.

'Sacha is a mature nineteen and you could do a lot worse. That actress, for instance, who was plastered all over you at that première. What was her name?'

Mathieu, not explaining it had been a stunt staged to gain

publicity for a low-budget movie, dismissed the young starlet with a contemptuous shrug and admitted, 'I have not the faintest idea.'

She had been and still was a total stranger, despite her offer to show him how grateful she was, a proposal he had said thanks, but no, thanks to.

His taste had never run to that sort of gratitude. The formula-one racing circuit attracted groupies like a magnet. Women who in his opinion represented everything that was bad about today's depressing shallow, celebrity-obsessed society.

Mathieu had frequently been tempted to say to them, Go away, get a life, get some self-respect, but he hadn't—any attention at all they took as encouragement. So he had gained a reputation for being aloof and unapproachable. He had changed careers but the reputation persisted. It was on occasion useful.

'I read the wedding plans were at an advanced stage.'

Mathieu angled a dark brow at the sarcasm in his father's voice and retorted lightly, 'I should review the sort of newspapers you read if I were you, Andreos.'

'You are not me.'

'Nor even a paler version.' He knew he took after his mother; he wondered sometimes if looking at him reminded his father of the young woman he had used and discarded.

'So there is no one—you are not in love?'

Mathieu was not in love or actively seeking it. On the contrary, if he saw it coming he had every intention of running or at least walking swiftly in the opposite direction.

What was the all-consuming attraction of love anyway? A form of temporary insanity that made your happiness reliant on someone else's smile?

The allure baffled him.

And anyway, the people he loved had a habit of dying.

No, falling in love was not on Mathieu's list of things to do.

The only person he relied on was himself and that was the way he liked it.

'I fail to see what business that is of yours, regardless of which I can think of few worse fates than to be married to a teenager, even a mature teenager.'

Andreos's face darkened with displeasure. 'I am not telling you to marry the girl.'

'But you wouldn't exactly be displeased if I did either, and in the meantime you will take every opportunity to throw us together. You are embarrassingly transparent.'

Andreos looked at him, his face dark with frustration. 'The girl is Vasilis's only child, his heir. Her husband would—'

Mathieu lifted a hand to still the flow. 'I hardly need it spelt out; you are empire-building.' His lips thinned in distaste. 'Does the girl have any say in this?'

'Do not look down your nose at me,' Andreos barked. 'And do not pretend you could not make this girl love you if you chose to do so. I have seen you with women.'

'She is not a woman; she is a child.'

'She was good enough for your brother.'

'They were in love.'

'You have taken everything else of his—why not his woman?'

The words hung in the air, building the tension between the two men, until Mathieu shrugged. 'I never wanted anything of Alex's.'

Except a share of their father's love, but that desire had only lasted until Mathieu was sixteen. He had been living with his father for a year when an overheard conversation had made him recognise that was never going to happen.

Mathieu's thoughts drifted back to the occasion in question. He had been walking past a half-open door. It was hearing his own name and the anger and frustration in his normally softly spoken stepmother's voice that had made him pause outside...

'The boy tries *so* hard, does everything you ask of him and more. Could you not just occasionally give him a word of en-couragement? Would it kill you, Andreos, to smile at him? All Mathieu wants is your approval. He's desperate for it. I can see it in his eyes when he looks at you. It breaks my heart.'

'What you see in his eyes is naked ambition, Mia. Why can you not see that? The boy is hard, he is confrontational—'

'You say you wish that Alex would stand up to you more.'

'That is not the same thing. Mathieu doesn't need love and kisses; he needs a strong hand.'

'Not one raised in anger, I have told you that. If you ever—'

'No, of course not. I told you I was sorry about that, Mia. You know I have never raised a hand to Alex; it's just Mathieu lied and then, caught out in the lie, refused to apologise.'

'Oh, for pity's sake, Andreos, are you blind? It was Alex who broke your precious statuette and he was too scared to own up so Mathieu took the blame.'

'No, no, you're wrong! I don't know what story he has told you, but—'

'Not Mathieu, he didn't say a word. It was Alex who told me about the beating and the broken statuette.'

'Oh, goddamn that boy…he made me…the thing is, Mia, when he looks at me all I can think is that I wish he'd never been born.'

He had heard enough. Mathieu had moved on, in more ways than one. It had hurt at the time to hear the truth, but it was better to face bitter reality than live in false hope.

'You will have to pass on my apologies. I'm expected in Scotland.'

A dark mottled colour rose up the older man's neck until his face was suffused with angry colour. Mathieu watched the effect of his words with clinical detachment.

The truth of it was he had returned just over a year ago at his stepmother's request, not his father's. 'Give it a year, Mathieu,' she begged. 'Your father needs you, though he'd never admit it.'

Mathieu was reluctant to shatter the illusion that he cared what his father needed, especially when she added, 'And when I am gone he will need you even more. The company and the family,' she reflected with a rueful roll of her eyes as she spoke of the Demetrios clan. 'They both need a strong hand at the helm. He was grooming your brother for the role…'

A memory had surfaced in Mathieu's head—Alexander sliding his small hand in his and saying earnestly, 'I want to be just like you when I am older, Mathieu, even if it means Father doesn't like me.'

'Alex would have done it well,' Mathieu lied.

Mia smiled and shook her head. 'I appreciate your loyalty, but we both know that isn't true. Alex hated business. He tried, of course, to please his father, but…' She shrugged. 'One day Andreos would have had to accept that Alex would never take his place, but sadly for us all that day never came.'

As Mathieu moved to enfold her in a comforting embrace, hiding his shock at the fragility of her birdlike frame, she grasped his hand tight and said fiercely, 'Promise me, Mathieu, to help him even if he doesn't want your help.'

So Mathieu had promised, and he had stayed after his promise to her had been fulfilled, not out of a sense of duty, but because against all the odds he was enjoying what he was doing.

'You ingrate, you will do as I say or…or…' Andreos raised his clenched fists from his sides and glared at the younger man with every appearance of loathing.

Mathieu, his calmness increasing in direct proportion to his father's furious incoherence, raised a satirical brow. 'You will disinherit me?' he suggested.

'And do not think I won't.'

'That is your decision.'

'You expect me to believe you don't care?' Andreos let out a loud bellow of scornful laughter and shook his head. 'That you don't care about losing an empire worth billions?'

'I don't ask you to believe anything,' Mathieu responded calmly. 'Your empire is yours to give to whom you wish. I know you wanted to give it to Alex—'

'Don't you dare say his name. He was worth ten of you.'

Mathieu continued seamlessly in the same even voice as though there had been no interruption. 'That is no longer possible. Alex is dead.' An image of his half-brother's smiling face flashed into his head and for a moment his sense of loss was so acute that he could not speak.

Alex, the indulged and adored only son, could have, should have, resented the bastard older brother who had suddenly appeared like a cuckoo in the gold-lined nest. But he had not. Alex's disposition had been as sunny and generous as his smile.

'I am the only son you have left,' he said bleakly. 'You wish to mould me into someone you think is fit to carry on your line.' Mathieu's smile revealed his total lack of regard for the illustrious family name he had inherited in his mid-teens. He had deliberately chosen to use his mother's name when he began his racing career to distance himself from that name.

'Well, I think we owe one another some honesty. I am not interested in your name, your line…your empire. I have a name of my own, and I am not some malleable child, Father. I was moulded, for better or worse, into what I am today a long time ago.'

The ruddy colour on the older man's cheeks deepened to an alarming purple. 'It is not my fault I did not know you existed…your mother…I brought you into my home after her death.'

Like a surgical knife Mathieu's deep, clear voice cut across the older man's blustering protest. 'Her name was Felicite, and you will not speak of my mother. You lost that right years ago.'

The older man's jaw dropped. He was not accustomed to being on the receiving end of commands. Nor was he used to seeing the glow of passion in the eyes of the son he had not known existed until he was fifteen years old.

'I gave you everything…'

Except love. 'I am not the son you want.' Mathieu gave a philosophical shrug. 'And you are not the father I would have chosen. But the fact is,' he continued calmly, 'I am the only son you have.'

The older Greek flinched as though struck and Mathieu added in a softer voice, 'We both wish it otherwise.'

Anger flared in the older man's eyes. 'Wish it otherwise?' he echoed, his lips twisted in a scornful grimace. 'Your brother being killed as he was left you the sole heir…yes, your tears were most apparent at the time,' he observed bitterly.

This was a subject they had tiptoed along the edge of many times and this time, like the others, it was Mathieu who drew back, though emotion surfaced and flared for a moment like silver fire in his heavy-lidded eyes before he responded with a moderate, 'We both wish it otherwise but this is the situation we find ourselves in. I suggest we both learn to live with it.'

'How dare you speak to me this way?'

Mathieu had learnt the hard way that showing emotion gave people the upper hand, but for once his iron control slipped and his emotions spilled out. 'You mean not like the puppet dancing to your tune?'

Andreos visibly recoiled from the blaze of fury written in every line of his son's patrician features. 'I have given you everything.'

'And everything you gave was given out of a sense of reluctant duty. You tolerate me only because it was Mia's dying wish. Has it not occurred to you…Father, that my actions are similarly constrained?'

It was clear from the older man's expression that he had not.

'She was always kind to me even though my very existence must have caused her pain.' He sucked in air through his flared nostrils and fought to regain his control. 'And it is only in respect of her wishes that I did not leave after her death.'

Both men were silent as they simultaneously recalled the last painful months of her life, which Mia had endured with cheerful dignity that had humbled those who had been lucky enough to be around her.

'As far as I am concerned the only thing you ever had going for you was the fact that a woman like that could love you. She must have seen something in you that I have not.'

'I will be leaving for Scotland tomorrow. You must do as you wish, Father…'

CHAPTER TWO

HER family's and friends' opinions were unanimous; Rose had lost her mind. Only a total lunatic, they reasoned, would leave a comfortable life in the capital where she had friends, family and a stimulating job she enjoyed to bury herself miles away from anything that remotely resembled civilisation, not to mention any place that served a halfway decent coffee.

Her twin sister had been particularly vocal in her opposition. In fact, initially Rebecca had been unable to believe her twin was serious about the move. Then, faced with the black-and-white reality of her sister's letter of resignation, she had stopped being amused and adopted a firm manner.

'This is a massive overreaction, Rose. You fell in love with your boss.' She lifted her slender shoulders in a so-what shrug. 'Who hasn't?'

Rose winced at the casual reference to Steven Latimer, protesting, 'Becky!' as her twin, who did dramatic with style, ripped up the letter and held out her hands as though her action settled the matter.

And Rose could see why she might think so. It was a classic case of someone believing their own press. Since they were children, people had been calling the more flamboyant Rebecca the dominant twin. It was probably only Rebecca's husband, Nick, who recognised the true dynamics of the twins' relationship.

'Sure, Rose gives in to Becky, but haven't you noticed it's only on the little things?' the shrewd New Yorker had observed. 'Things that don't actually matter. When it comes to something important, that she cares about, Rose could give a mule lessons in stubborn, though you don't realise it because she says no with such a sweet smile.' He had flashed his sister-in-law one of his own laconic smiles and winked.

At that moment—Rebecca had dragged him along to convince Rose of the error of her ways—he earned himself a black look by observing when appealed to for support by his wife that it was pretty much up to Rose what she did.

Rose would have been more grateful if he hadn't added, for the record, that, yes, he did think that Steven Latimer was a lower form of human life.

Rose glared at her brother-in-law and picked up a piece of torn paper from the floor. 'All I have to do is print out another copy, Becky.'

'Is this about Latimer, Rosie?' Nick interrupted. 'Are you leaving because he is putting pressure on you? Because you don't have to put up with it, honey. Nowadays employers take a very dim view of sexual harassment.'

Rose shook her head firmly. 'Steven isn't like that, Nick. He's a very honourable man.'

'I wonder if your marvellous Steven would be quite so honourable if his wife wasn't the boss's daughter?'

'Becky, that's not fair.'

'Was it fair of him to tell you he was desperately in love with you?'

'It wasn't something he planned.'

'In my opinion Steven Latimer plans everything. The man hasn't a spontaneous bone in his body—which I admit isn't bad.

He's also the most calculating person I've ever met…and I've met a few.'

'Steven might come over as a little ambitious sometimes.'

Her twin didn't mince her words. 'He'd sell his grandmother for a seat on the board.'

'He went to Eton with a guy I know.'

Rose turned her head at the interruption. 'Eton?' Anyone else she might have accused of lying, but her brother-in-law was as straight as they came. 'No, your friend must be mistaken. Steven went to an inner-city state school.'

'Is that what he told you?' Rebecca snorted, bending to pick up the shredded paper from the rug. Looking at her twin, she began to thread it between the perfectly manicured fingers of her right hand.

'Why would he lie?'

'Because he isn't a nice man. The man you fell in love with only exists in your head, Rose,' Rebecca said, tapping the side of her own blonde head with its new gamine crop. 'He's a self-serving bastard and you're such a hopeless romantic.' She sighed. 'You know, I think you prefer a tragic unrequited love because it's safer than the real thing—you're a coward, Rose!'

Rose shook her head. This had been a hard decision to make but she knew it was the right one, no matter how Rebecca tried to twist things.

'I've always wanted to go to the Scottish Highlands,' she reminded her sister.

'*Go*, not *live*,' Rebecca exploded, running a frustrated hand over the hair. 'I can't believe you're actually serious.'

'I just need a break. This man needs his book collection catalogued. I only fell into the marketing job. I originally trained as a librarian—'

Rebecca gave an impatient snort. 'Don't try and pretend this is about musty old books, because we both know it isn't. You're running away; it's a big mistake. For God's sake, it's not like anything happened…' She stopped and gave her sister a sharp look. 'Is it…?'

'He's married.'

Rose's outraged expression had seemed to amuse her sister. 'It has been known, Rose, for married people to have affairs,' she taunted gently. 'You do know you're something of a rarity in the twenty-first century, don't you?'

Rose had been stung by her sister's affectionate mockery. 'Because I won't sleep with a married man?'

'No, actually that doesn't make you totally unique—even with my colourful history I might have a few qualms about that.'

Despite the levity in her sister's tone Rose knew that she had strayed on sensitive ground. Rebecca could be pretty touchy about what she liked to call her 'summer to forget'. It was a subject that by tacit agreement neither referred to.

'Sorry, I didn't mean that you're…'

'That I'm an abandoned hussy?' Rebecca suggested with a twinkle. 'Relax, Rosie, Nick knows all about my chequered history, don't you, darling?'

Her tall husband stretched laconically and offered her a lopsided grin with his nod of wry agreement. 'A paragraph,' he announced with a hint of complacence. 'My past would fill several volumes.'

Behind his teasing there was profound love and commitment that brought an emotional lump to Rose's throat. Her sister had found the man of her dreams too. Why couldn't Rebecca recognise that the only difference between them was that Nick had been available?

Was everything in life merely down to timing?

'The Scottish Highlands! You know I can't believe you're actually serious about this. You're mad, totally insane!'

* * *

Rose had defended her sanity but as a second sickening splintering sound issued from under her feet and the crack in the ice spread rapidly she was forced to consider the very real possibility Rebecca might have had a point.

Mathieu had risen early, long before anyone else in the house was awake. He enjoyed solitude, time to recharge his batteries and gather his thoughts without the distractions of phones and faxes, but moments like this one had become increasingly rare over the past months.

Not that he was complaining. Against all the odds he found he loved what he was doing, and he was learning all the time.

It was a steep learning curve, but he relished the challenge and knew that even if it ultimately proved impossible for him to work with Andreos he would take these new skills with him when he left.

And, on a less charitable note, in the meantime he had the pleasure of knowing Andreos, who had never disguised the fact that he didn't think his bastard son had what it took, was struggling to hide his frustration when he hadn't fallen flat on his face.

Yet, he corrected himself with a mocking grin. You know what they say about pride and falls, Mathieu.

Someone had recently asked if he hadn't found the restrictions of riding a desk after the freedom of the racing circuit crushing. They had not understood why he had laughed, but like many they hadn't had the faintest idea of the sort of physical and mental discipline both required to compete at the level he had.

They saw the glamour but not the struggle to remain at the peak in a competitive environment.

He slipped his rucksack from one shoulder to the other and rotated his neck to ease the tension that still remained in his shoulders. The chair in Jamie's study was not designed with human posture in mind and he had worked long into the night, poring over the accounts, a flattering description for the collection of papers and illegible scribbles in the ledgers that Jamie had supplied him with.

They did not make for happy reading. Far from exaggerating the situation as he had suspected, Jamie had if anything underplayed the seriousness of his position.

It had been dawn when he had tackled the climb so, with any luck—his glance skimmed his watch—yes, he ought to make it back in time for breakfast and to place a few calls.

The post-climb general sense of well-being combined with the dregs of the adrenaline rush were still circulating in his blood as he made his way to the spot where he had parked the Land Rover. He glanced once more at the metal-banded watch on his wrist and quickened his pace already planning his strategy, though he suspected it would come down in the end to plan B...it was always good to have a plan B.

He was about half a mile from the Land Rover when movement in the periphery of his vision made him turn his head in time to see a red-hatted figure moving below. Someone else who enjoyed the morning, he thought, moving off again. He had reached a steep slope of scree directly above the loch when some instinct made him stop and seek out the distant figure.

'Nobody is that stupid...' He held his breath for a moment as the figure stepped out onto what he knew to be paper-thin ice.

He hit the ground running. He didn't waste his breath shouting, knowing the person below would never hear him above the wind that whistled through the valley.

He was fifty yards away when the stillness was rent first by a loud cracking sound, then a woman's scream. A final sprint brought him to the edge of the ice in seconds.

A girlfriend had once accused him of having too little imagination to be sensibly scared of anything, but she was wrong.

He just saw little benefit under the circumstances of wasting time to linger on the lurid details of death by drowning in cold, icy water. Instead as he pulled off his light padded outer jacket he scanned the ice estimating his chances.

His actions were swift but not hurried, his brain working out all the factors. It was his ability to think clearly in situations like this that had made him a successful racing driver. That combined with lightning reflexes, nerves of steel and, according to some of his competitors, more than his fair share of ruthless cunning.

Mathieu didn't think of it in those terms, but he did know that his thought processes were at their sharpest when the stakes were high. Right now they were as high as they got—a life.

The situation did not allow for further preliminary evaluation so, sucking in a breath, he tucked his ice axe into the belt of his trousers and lay down flat on his belly to distribute his weight as evenly as possible on the thin ice. Then Mathieu began to crawl as quickly as possible towards the hole that stood like a gaping black wound in the silvered surface of the frozen water.

He saw the top of a red hat surface, heard the stifled yell and pushed himself faster regardless of the warning creaks of the fragile ice underneath him. He reached the edge of the gash in the ice in time to see the white hand vanish beneath the water.

He hauled himself to the edge of the hole and thrust his ice axe into the water. Relief flooded through him as it snagged on something. His face set in lines of grim determination, the sinews in his neck pulling taut, he began to pull.

Even as she opened her mouth to scream for help Rose was very aware that the chance of anyone being around to hear her was, at the most optimistic, remote.

The second scream of visceral fear remained locked in her throat as the ice beneath her feet opened up and she fell. She had never imagined that cold could be this extreme. It enveloped her, freezing the air in her lungs, its icy tentacles infiltrating every cell of her body. After the first paralysing shock she began to struggle, kicking out wildly in panic as she fought her way to the surface.

Rose was a good swimmer but the extremely low temperature of the water sapped her strength within minutes.

'Help me,' she screamed as she felt herself sliding beneath the surface. Cocooned in the icy darkness, aware only of the heavy thud of her own heartbeat as it continued to pump the oxygen-starved blood around her body, she refused to accept the inevitable.

I am not going to drown.

But she was.

Still Rose refused to accept the reality of it. Clinging stubbornly to the last flicker of hope, she kicked weakly for the surface even though she knew she wasn't going to make it.

Only she did. Just as she had used up the last reserves of strength and her lungs were burning she felt something snag in her coat, then she was being dragged upwards.

Holding the bedraggled girl's head above the icy water, Mathieu could just about make out her muffled words. The damsel in distress had reached the inevitable 'what happened?' phase. He didn't waste his breath replying, though if she asked, 'Who am I?' he would have a harder time restraining himself. People called him a risk-taker, but any risks he took were of the clear-headed, calculated variety. If this girl wasn't suicidal to pull a stunt like this she was...she had to be one of the most criminally stupid women ever to draw breath!

'It is important to stay calm and not struggle,' Rose heard the deep voice above her say.

Struggle. Was he joking? At the moment breathing required all her energy and each raw breath she dragged in through blue lips hurt.

'When I pull you clear...'

Now that sounded like a good idea. It was also good that he

hadn't suggested she do this herself as her limbs were not responding to any requests; she couldn't even feel them.

'I'm just going to—'

'Wait!' Rose protested, lifting her head in panic as she felt herself pushed briefly clear of the relative security of the ice. 'N-no…don't.'

Her warning went unheeded.

'I'm just going to put this rope around you. It's all right, just be still.'

Rose felt the rope her rescuer had just looped under her arms tighten.

'That's it, you're perfectly safe now.' Mathieu said this with a confidence he did not feel.

He shot a glance over his shoulder towards the shore and safety. As he had crawled out there had been several moments when the ice underneath him had threatened to give way.

She could feel the heat of her rescuer's breath on her icy cheek as he bent closer. Her nostrils flared in response to the clean male scent of his body overlaid with a light citrusy scent. He represented safety but she really felt she ought to warn him that pulling her out of the water might not be so easy.

'S…s…seven to ten p…pounds…' Shut up, Rose, you sound unbalanced.

'Seven…?'

'Doesn't matter.' Still, it would be kind of ironic in a dark sort of way if the amount of excess the magazines said she needed to shed if she wanted any shot at happiness in this world was the amount that tipped the balance.

What if her determination not to end up a victim to the prevailing fashion for unrealistically thin women ended up being the reason for her demise?

She laughed and above her a man's voice advised her once more to stay calm. She opened her mouth to tell him she wasn't the type to have hysterics when the ice gave another loud warning creak and she changed her mind.

Perhaps she was the type to have hysterics? Under these circumstances perhaps everyone was the type. Then she remembered the sound of her rescuer's deep, calm voice, and thought maybe he was the exception, which was lucky for her.

The situation was better than he had dared hope—there were no new major cracks visible. However, only an insane optimist would expect this situation to last for long. The window of opportunity for this rescue was small.

He took a deep breath and, totally focused on the task ahead, smiled slightly. He knew what he had to do; there were no fuzzy lines, no protocol or politics to consider. It was a simple matter of survival; these were factors he felt comfortable working with.

Mathieu braced his knees on the thin ice beside the woman who had given a scared whimper. 'Let's do this.' She had reason to be scared. He probably ought to be, but the adrenaline pumping in his bloodstream sharpened his reactions and dulled his caution.

Do what? Rose thought.

'Are you ready?'

Roused by the sheer inanity of this comment, Rose lifted her head. 'No, I'm not ready!' The indignation died from her face as her full lower lip quivered. 'I don't want to die…' Her voice trailed away as her eyes connected with those of her rescuer.

They were the palest grey, almost silver, slanted upwards in the corners, the heavy lids fringed by long, curling, sooty lashes. Even this close to descending into gibbering fear she registered in some portion of her brain that they were the most excruciatingly beautiful eyes she had ever seen in her life.

The sort of eyes that a doctor might prescribe for someone who had just had a near-death experience to look into: beautiful. The rest of his face was a blur as she concentrated on those beautiful eyes, but she had the impression of sharp angles and intriguing hollows.

There was a fractional pause before he responded calmly and for a moment she imagined she saw something flicker in the silvered enigmatic depths...*recognition*...? Which made no sense, because if she had ever met a man with those eyes she would not have forgotten!

'Nobody is going to die. I'm going to lift you out of the water.'

He made it sound so easy. She nodded, thinking again of that seven to ten pounds. 'What do you want me to—? Oh!' The breath huffed out of her chest in a noisy gasp as she landed face down on the ice. She lay there and felt the tears leak from her eyes. 'I'm not going to drown.'

'Not if you do exactly what I say,' came the not exactly comforting response. 'Are you injured? Do you have pain?'

She lifted her head, wiping the water-darkened strands of hair from her cheek...the shore seemed an awful long way away. She shook her head. 'Just cold and tired. If I could just rest for a minute...'

A hand under her chin jerked her head up. 'Open your eyes. Now!'

She obeyed the imperative command and saw the man with the beautiful eyes was totally unmoved by the tears that welled up in her own eyes. She blinked; she wasn't after a sympathy vote.

As her misty vision cleared she registered properly several more details of her rescuer's appearance beyond his spectacular eyes. The hair that waved smoothly back from a broad brow and fell silky straight to his collar—had he been wearing one—was dark. The sable shade echoed in his dark winged eyebrows was complemented by a clear olive-toned complexion.

His patrician face was long with high, razor-sharp cheekbones and an angular jaw that was lightly dusted with a dark shadow of stubble. His nose was strong and aquiline and his mouth wide and mobile. Rose found the overtly sensual outline of his lips almost cruel.

He was the most incredibly good-looking male she had ever seen or even imagined and yet when she looked at him she found herself almost repelled by his male beauty. Well, what other emotion could be responsible for the uncomfortable, lurching, shivery sensation in her belly when she looked at his saturnine face?

'You will not fall asleep.'

Rose wanted to ask if he really thought she was that stupid. But she didn't have the energy and, besides, he probably did think just that. Instead she just nodded and asked, 'What do I do?'

'Keep flat, move slowly.'

'I'll try.'

'Trying is not good enough if you don't want to kill us both. I will be behind you, but it is most important that we distribute our weight evenly, stay low and flat…' he made a sweeping horizontal motion with one hand to indicate how he wanted her to move '…commando-style.'

'Commando?' Rose repeated, wondering if he did something along those lines for real.

Her glance skimmed the muscle-packed length of him. He had that lean, hard look that made it easy to imagine him being part of some élite group trained for covert operations. And then there was the air of authority. Not many people could give, let alone maintain, that kind of authority when lying belly down on thin ice!

'You understand?'

She nodded. 'But the rope…is it such a good idea…?' She looked from the rope looped around her waist and followed it to his washboard-flat middle. 'If anything goes wrong we are tied together.' She didn't want to be responsible for pulling this good Samaritan into the icy water.

'Then we shall just have to make very sure that nothing goes wrong, won't we?' he inserted with the impatient air of someone not used to having his instructions questioned. 'You are ready?'

She nodded, thinking there were some things a person was never ready for, but he had made it pretty clear she had very little choice.

The progress they made seemed torturously slow, though she knew it couldn't have taken as long as it felt. Each time she felt she could go no further because her legs were shaking or she just couldn't feel them her rescuer was there, encouraging her, though his encouragement at times bordered on coercion.

CHAPTER THREE

FINALLY on solid land, Rose simply lay there for several moments, too euphoric at being safe to even register the cold that every flutter of wind was driving deeper into her bones. Then, pulling her shaking knees up to her chest, she heaved herself into a sitting position, hugging her arms around her body.

The dark stranger was beside her. He had hunkered down to her level and was casually balancing on his heels with the inbred grace of a natural athlete.

'Thank you so much; you saved my life.'

She found it slightly off-putting that there was not a flicker of expression in the spooky silver-grey eyes trained on her face.

'I'm Rose, by the way, Mr…?'

Mathieu looked into the incredible amber eyes brimming with gratitude and innocent as a kitten, which could not be more different from the reckless, sexual challenge he recalled last seeing in those same eyes. If she intended to pretend they did not know one another it was nothing to him. He supposed it was *just* possible that she didn't—his upper lip curled in fastidious contempt—she had been very drunk that night.

The win had clinched him the champion's medal for the fourth year running. So for that reason alone the evening of the gala reception at the embassy would have lingered on in his memory, even if he hadn't returned to his hotel room later that night to find a naked woman in his bed.

A woman who had smooth skin like cream, long hair the colour of pale caramel and golden eyes.

The golden eyes that were looking at him now.

'Can you walk?'

She blinked at the abruptness of his question and the smile faded from her face. She was philosophical about the hostility in his manner. His life had just been put at risk because of her. He was bound not to look too kindly on the person responsible for his close encounter, although the level of cold disdain in his body language did seem excessive. He was looking at her as though she were something offensive on his shoe!

She attempted to struggle clumsily to her feet. 'Of course.'

Mathieu, who had realised the moment he had formed the question that she could probably barely feel her limbs, never mind walk, ignored her optimistic assertion and bent to scoop her up. As he gathered her to him he was aware first of softness, then, before he had time to wonder at the heat that exploded inside him—cold, icy cold.

A glance revealed her skin had an unhealthy bluish tinge, which was hardly surprising considering what she had been through. He was well aware of the danger of hypothermia. It was imperative that she warmed up quickly.

'I…what are you doing?' Rose stuttered as she found herself slung unceremoniously over his shoulder.

'Preventing you getting hypothermia. The Land Rover's parked just up on the track,' he explained, mentally assessing the time it would take him to reach it.

He didn't say anything. Not another word until they reached the vehicle, which did not surprise her. What man could speak with an overweight—and that was dry—blonde over his shoulder? What did surprise her was that he could keep up a brisk running pace the entire way and still not be breathing very hard.

Pulling open the door, Mathieu dumped his shaking burden in the back seat before going around to the driver's side and switching on the engine, sliding the thermostat on the heater to full.

'Get the wet things off.' He barely glanced in her direction before leaving the front of the Land Rover.

He returned a moment later carrying a metallic survival blanket and a heavy cable-knitted sweater, which he flung in the seat beside her. His dark brows drew into a straight line as he assessed her progress.

'Did you not hear me? I said take those things off,' he said, sliding into the driver's seat and turning around.

Heater on full, the cab was hot, but Rose was still shaking. She actually couldn't imagine ever stopping, ever being warm again. 'Sorry. My fingers,' she said, holding out the slim, pale tapering items under discussion apologetically; like the rest of her they were shaking. 'I can't f-feel them.'

His dark eyes slid from her face to her fingers. There was a tiny pause before he heaved a sigh that suggested exasperation. 'Then I suppose I'll have to do it for you.'

'Do what?' The dumb routine was a self-defence mechanism, because she knew if she let herself consider in any serious way what having this man remove her clothes, even in a totally clinical, I'm-saving-your-life sort of way, might feel like, she might do or say something terminally embarrassing.

There was a blast of cold air in response to her question, then another as the passenger door opened and he slid in beside her so close that their thighs touched and slammed the door shut.

The thigh beside her own had all the give of a steel bar. He was an extremely tall, athletically built man and pretty much all of him looked equally hard. He was the sort of man who could make an auditorium seem small!

This was not an auditorium, it was a hot, steamy tin box on wheels, and it wasn't just his physical presence that made it uncomfortable to share the enclosed space with him, it was the raw sensual energy that cloaked him like a second skin. Though she couldn't help noticing that his first skin was pretty special.

Embarrassed by the direction of her thoughts, she flicked a sideways glance at his classical profile, her nostrils quivering as she tried not to inhale the subtle male scent of his body. His presence made it impossible to concentrate on anything else but…well, anything but him!

He was totally overpowering and not at all, she reflected, trying to co-ordinate her actions, a comfortable man to be around. When their glances connected, his slightly impatient, she looked away biting her lip because she knew she was acting like some gauche schoolgirl.

For God's sake, Rose, anyone would think from the way you're acting that the man is trying to seduce you.

She swallowed and lifted her head determined to match his pragmatic manner as he shifted in his seat so that they were facing one another.

She suddenly laughed.

One dark brow lifted. 'What is so funny?'

She shook her head. 'Nothing.' It was hardly the right moment to inform him that she'd just realised this was the first time she'd been in the back seat of a car with a man.

Rebecca would say her education had been sadly neglected. Rebecca would probably have a point. Some people were simply not born with the reckless, exciting gene and she was one of them. Neither was she particularly highly sexed.

This man probably knew his way around the back seat of a car, she mused, studying his lean, autocratic face through the shield of her lashes, though he had probably moved on from the nursery slopes of fumbling long ago. Nowadays she doubted her imagination stretched to cover the things he could find his way around.

It was some comfort that he definitely didn't seem as if he wanted to do any of those things with her. She stared at his sinfully sexy mouth. Of course, she didn't want him to leap on her or anything, but she wouldn't mind knowing just once what it would feel like to be the sort of woman who made a man's mind turn to such things.

She could always ask Rebecca, who was such a woman, or maybe lose half a stone...? His terse voice broke into her rambling thoughts.

'Lift up your arms.'

Rose would have broken contact with those disturbing eyes if she could have but they exerted a strange, almost hypnotic hold.

'Look, this really won't be necessary.' She was dismayed to hear her voice emerge as a breathy whisper without a trace of the amused competence she had intended to inject into it. 'I'll change when I get home.'

To her consternation, instead of taking the opportunity to rid himself of her, his body language having made perfectly clear that was what he wanted, he sketched a cynical smile that lifted the corners of his wide mobile mouth.

'Don't worry, *yineka mou,* I'm quite willing to take it as read that you're incredibly modest.'

Rose was bewildered both by the smile and the distinct undercurrent of scorn in his voice. But the drawled endearment explained the fascinating but faint foreign inflection in his voice she would have puzzled over later when reliving the encounter.

He was Greek, and rude.

Her smile was warmer than it might have been because the latter observation made her feel pretty much an ungrateful wretch—if it hadn't been for this rude Greek she would most likely now be in a watery grave.

The acknowledgement sent a shiver, stronger than the others that intermittently overcame her, down the length of her spine. She looked at his mouth—it was frankly hard not to—and smiled without as much conviction this time because somehow she found his mouth deeply disturbing, and said, 'You're Greek?'

'Half Greek, half French…did you not read my bio?'

'Your bio…?' she parroted, no longer even trying to follow him.

She closed her eyes and leaned back with a weary sigh. Even though she was no longer looking at him she was still very aware of his presence. Considering she had only studied his features briefly, she appeared to have memorised every detail of his extraordinary face. Even with her eyes closed every strong angle and plane was etched into her brain.

'Most do,' he observed drily.

And having read all the stuff on the websites, and the reams of nonsense that were printed about him, these women thought they knew him.

He had never fathomed why these women were so drawn to celebrity; something, he reasoned, had to be missing in their own lives that they spent so much of their time fantasising about a total stranger.

'Sorry, I don't read as much as I'd like to. If you could just drop me off…' Her voice trailed off.

Curses sounded like curses in any language and presumably the ones that fell fluently from his lips would have made a less unrestrained Greek blush.

He dragged a hand through his dark hair and regarded her closed eyes with exasperation tinged by concern. 'You cannot fall asleep!'

'Sorry…no, of course.' Her blue-veined eyelids lifted as she gave her head a little shake. 'I'm really grateful, you know,' she told him as she tucked her hands under her legs. The circulation was returning to her fingers, and they were throbbing painfully.

'I think you saved my life,' she said, rocking forward as the throbbing intensified.

'What you did was criminally stupid.'

Rose bit her lip, but she supposed that under the circumstances he had earned the right to speak to her as though she were some not too bright child.

'I'd ask what you were thinking of, but clearly you weren't thinking.'

'There was a fox…' She could only assume that when the ice had cracked it had escaped, or maybe it had never even been stuck…?

'I saw no fox.' He dismissed the animal in question with a regal wave of his hand. Clearly he hadn't seen it, so it couldn't have been there—not a man who spent a lot of time agonising over self-doubt.

'Which doesn't mean it wasn't there,' she pointed out.

'I saw no animal.' Just a woman determined, it seemed, to end her life. Mathieu relived the moment he had seen her vanish beneath the icy water and his simmering anger surged. 'What sort of person would walk out onto paper-thin ice to rescue a *fox*?'

The sort of person who had to switch channels when there was a wildlife programme where the makers did not intervene—and they could have—even though the weak, injured or just unlucky animal was about to meet a slow, lingering or occasionally violent and savage end.

She could have explained this, but she doubted he would be interested. Clearly what he wanted, and given the circumstances deserved, was a grovelling apology along the lines of, 'I'm insane and you're incredible.' Which he was if your taste ran to macho alpha males.

'If this was some sort of stunt to get my attention again…? It worked.'

'Stunt?' she echoed, blinking up at him. 'Again?' she added, her voice lifted in confused enquiry.

'I'm assuming this act is because I hurt your pride?'

'*Pride…?*' She was too confused to do anything more than echo what he said as she met his laserlike stare warily. The man really did have eyes that looked as though they could see into your skull and read your thoughts, which was disturbing because some of the thoughts that popped into her head when she looked at him were not ones she would have felt comfortable sharing.

Least of all with the person they concerned.

Did he inspire lust in all women he met or was she particularly susceptible? Maybe a person could only suppress their libido for so long before it rebelled?

'When I threw you out,' he prompted. It was a pity she had not displayed a little of this pride when she had offered herself to him.

Her eyes widened. 'Threw me out…?'

'Of my hotel room, my bed…'

Her jaw hit her chest and for a moment she forgot about her throbbing fingers. 'Why would I be in your room or…' she swallowed and gulped '…bed? I don't even know you.'

'Look, I'm willing to humour you and pretend if that is what you wish—we've never met before, OK.' The scornful smile that twisted his lips vanished as he added, 'But I'm not willing to let you die of hypothermia, not after all the effort to get you out of the loch.'

Rose swallowed. He really did have the hardest eyes she had ever seen. 'I think you must have mistaken me for someone else.' She struggled not to show her concern.

Had she just got into a car with a dangerous lunatic? It was starting to seem like a strong possibility.

A hissing sound of exasperation escaped his white, clenched teeth. 'Look, if you want to pretend you did not bribe your way into my hotel room, that is fine by me, and I'm not suggesting for a moment that you don't do this gushing, sweet, innocent act very well,' he conceded nastily. 'But it might be more productive if you save it for a man who hasn't seen you naked.'

'What? Naked?' Her hands came up in a protective gesture across her breasts. It would take a woman who was either very brave, or very beautiful, to parade naked in front of a man as physically perfect as this man.

And she was not that woman.

'You have never seen me naked.' It didn't matter how many near-death experiences she had, that was something she would not have forgotten.

'Well, if you're going to be pedantic I wasn't counting the stockings and stilettos.'

The visual image in her head that accompanied his husky concession sent the mortified blood rushing to her cold cheeks. 'Look at me.' Her shrill invitation was unnecessary because he already was and not in a way she liked. 'I've never worn stockings in my life, not even hold-ups…' He's accusing you of being a predatory tart and you take the time to tackle the stockings issue—sure, that makes perfect sense, Rose.

'I do not forget a face or a body,' he added, his eyes dropping to the upper slopes of her full creamy breasts. 'Your body has…ripened,' he admitted. 'And the blush is a new addition to your repertoire…it's good.'

'I do not have a repertoire.' The smouldering sexual insolence in his bold stare started a chain reaction that began low in her belly. In a matter of seconds her entire body was involved. If she hadn't been sitting down her legs would have folded under her. She couldn't believe that she had reacted this way to a casually lecherous stare.

'The weight suits you.' The woman in his bed at the hotel had possessed the lean, angular, borderline androgynous build that models aspired to. It had crossed his mind at the time that she would have undoubtedly looked more attractive with her clothes on.

The same could not be said now.

'Look, you've had your joke, but enough is enough,' she said,

even though one look at his expression made it clear he hadn't.
It seemed probable, going on what she had seen of him so far,
that he wouldn't know a joke if he fell over it.

'We've never met, I promise you.'

'I've encountered a lot of groupies but you stood out.'

'Groupie...' Best to treat this all as a joke. Co-operate, keep
him happy and the quicker she'd be back at Dornie House, and
after that she'd never have to see this man again.

She wasn't getting very far with denial so she tried a different tack. 'Sure, I eat men like you before breakfast.' Her mocking
grin slipped as an erotic image flashed into her head.

A man, his face hidden by the curtain of hair of the woman
who sat astride him, lying naked on the tumbled silken bed-
clothes of a vast bed. His fingers were wound into the bars of a
metal headboard and entwined with those of the woman. Deep
fractured moans were issuing from his throat as the bed creaked
under their combined weight. The woman's hair fell back and...

Rose sucked in a sharp breath. Oxygen starvation, that was
the only explanation she could think of for the lurid erotic fantasy
that had crawled out of her subconscious.

'But you'll be pleased to hear that drowning has had a damp-
ening effect on my libido.'

Mathieu, dragging his eyes from the heaving outline of
her breasts, swallowed. It was a pity he could not say the same
for his own libido. He could only assume it was the adrenaline
that was still circulating in his blood now the danger was
past...though adrenaline caused a flight-or-fight reaction and he
felt no compelling urge to do either.

'It's put me right off my daily diet of reluctant men. So you're
quite safe.'

He gave a triumphant smile. 'So you admit that you are that
woman.'

She clamped her lips together. 'No, I damned well don't.'

'There's no need to yell. Your secret is safe with me. Relax.'

Was he mad? 'Would you relax if someone suggested you were their rejected one-night stand?'

'What do you object to—the one-night-stand tag or the rejection? And for the record I do not do one-night stands.'

She saw the spark of anger in his eyes and thought, Great, it's all right for him to take offence. 'That's what I'm saying, neither do I. I don't…' She stopped, remaining immobile as he bent forward and unzipped her jacket.

He lifted his head and their eyes connected. Without a word he slid it off her shoulders.

'Lift up your arms.'

Without thinking Rose obeyed his command this time and her sodden sweater was peeled away. Brushing a heavy hank of water-darkened caramel-blonde hair from her eyes, she looked at the sweater as it fell onto the floor of the Land Rover. The tee shirt she had worn underneath had come away with it.

She was sitting there stripped to the waist in nothing but what felt like acres of bare goose-pimpled flesh and her pink lace bra that had definitely seen better days. She saw his eyes drop and like a tide the hot, mortified colour washed over her skin.

Mathieu's gaze slid upwards over her body. By the time he reached her heavy breasts encased in a light lacy bra through which the dark circles of her nipples were clearly visible the dull throb of blood in his temples had become a pounding roar.

Every instinct Rose possessed made her want to cover herself but that would be as good as saying she was not comfortable with her own body, that she had something to be ashamed of, whereas it was him, the sleaze, she thought wrathfully, who should feel guilty for ogling.

'I thought you'd seen it all before,' she snapped when the moment of paralysing embarrassment had passed.

His head came up with a jerk. Rose registered the dark

colour scoring the crests of his sculpted cheekbones and then their eyes connected.

His smoky stare sent a fresh quiver of sexual awareness through her body. This had to be about the near-death experience; she didn't react like this to men…not even Steven. And they had worked in close proximity most days.

Very close sometimes, which was part of the reason she had left. But a small part, because she had never feared not being able to control herself. The real reason was she felt guilty, ashamed because she had feelings for a married man.

If she had to work with this man on a daily basis, have his hand brush hers, feel his breath on her neck as he bent over her desk to read a report as Steven had done many times…? Rose shuddered. The horrifying imaginary scenario made her want to crawl out of her skin.

'Don't be embarrassed. The extra padding has gone to all the right places.'

Padding! Rose gritted her teeth. She was comfortable with her weight. She knew she was never going to be a size eight, basically because she would never starve herself and become a gym junkie like Rebecca to achieve it, but there was a line. And he had just crossed it.

She embraced the anger, gritting her teeth, and gave him a steady look. 'You're too kind.'

'No, I'm not. I'm not kind at all.'

Looking into his spooky pale eyes, Rose believed him. She shivered and lowered her gaze.

CHAPTER FOUR

IGNORING him as best she could, Rose pulled the heavy dry sweater over her head. It reached her knees and acted as a screen as, still shaking feverishly, she peeled away her jeans.

Before she had managed to wriggle them down to her ankles he had opened the door and returned to the front seat without a word. He started the engine with a curt instruction for her to belt up.

*Belt up…*he probably, she decided, meant it in both senses of the word, which was no problem for her. The last thing she felt like was making conversation. They'd been driving for a couple of minutes before she realised he couldn't know where she lived.

'I'm staying at Dornie House, that's the last turning after—'

His impatient voice cut across her. 'I'm not taking you there.' His eyes met hers in the rear-view mirror. 'You need to get checked over; there's a cottage hospital in Muir.'

'I don't need to see a doctor.'

'Need or not, you're going to,' came the autocratic retort.

Short of jumping out a moving vehicle, she didn't have much choice but to go along with his plan. The man was obviously a total control freak.

'There's a blanket on the back seat if you don't mind a few dog hairs. It should only take five minutes or so.'

She lasted three. She was wasting her breath, she knew that, but how could she let him go away thinking that she was someone she wasn't? She really wanted to hear him admit he was wrong.

'I've never slept with you, you know.' Or anyone else, though Rebecca's theory on this sad state of affairs was wrong—it wasn't because she was a hopeless romantic who couldn't deal with real emotions. That was the problem. She *wanted* emotions; she didn't want soulless sex.

It was just her luck that the one man she had met whom she could imagine sex not being a cold, mechanical exercise with had already been taken. Her brow wrinkled as she recalled Rebecca's suggestion that it wasn't accidental she had fallen in love with someone who was inaccessible. Then she found herself recalling that one time when Steven had kissed her…it hadn't been what she had expected. She hadn't been carried away by passion; in fact, she had felt oddly removed from the event.

'Only because I threw you out.'

His scornful observation cut like a blade through Rose's rambling reflections.

'Why? What was wrong with me?' Rose closed her eyes and bit her lip… Could I have sounded more like a rejected lover if I tried?

'I do not sleep with drunk groupies,' he announced with disdainful hauteur.

The blood that had returned to her tingling extremities now rushed to her head. 'Now hang on, I know you probably saved my life, but—'

He cut across her with a sardonic, 'Probably?'

'All right, then,' she conceded crossly. 'You saved my life, but that doesn't give you the right to invent stories and virtually call me a tramp.'

'It was not a term I used, but what would *you* call a woman who targets famous men with the purpose of adding another scalp to her belt? An icon of modern female empowerment?'

'Famous?' she echoed, getting seriously angry. 'Am I supposed to know who you are?'

Dark brows elevated to an incredulous angle, he shot her a look of sardonic amusement in the rear-view mirror. 'You are trying to tell me you don't?'

'I have never laid eyes on you before today,' she snapped angrily.

'Fine.' He sighed, sounding like someone who was bored but prepared to go through the motions for a quiet life. 'I am Mathieu Gauthier…'

Of course she knew the name even though she didn't follow formula one. Well, it explained the arrogance—the adulation those drivers got was ludicrous. He had probably started believing his press releases.

'Is that meant to mean something?'

It was obvious from the brief look he slung her over his shoulder that he didn't swallow her pretended ignorance for a second, but to her relief he didn't challenge her lie, but sounded lazily amused as he said, 'If you are a fan of formula one it might.'

'I thought you were Greek. *Gauthier* doesn't sound very Greek to me.'

The lazy smile faded from his face. 'Half Greek. I used my mother's name professionally.'

'So you are actually…?'

'Mathieu Demetrios. Look, you don't need to do this. I'm not going to tell anyone if that's what is worrying you. Maybe your life has moved on and you're ashamed of your past…though in my opinion you'd do better to come clean with whoever is in your life now.' He didn't doubt for a moment there would be somebody; for women who looked as she did there was always somebody.

'Thank you for the advice,' she gritted, thinking it was so not asked for. 'But I'm not ashamed. I have nothing in my past to be ashamed of.' *Which makes me one of the most sad twenty-six-*

year-olds on the planet. 'I don't even know where or when I'm supposed to have tried to…to…seduce you.'

'Monaco.'

'Well, I've never been to Mon—' She stopped. She hadn't, but Rebecca had. She had the postcard to prove it.

Rose closed her eyes, a silent sigh leaving her lips. The woman he was talking about, sneering at, the woman who had tried to seduce him, was none other than her twin.

Rebecca who had been dumped literally at the altar and gone a little crazy. It all fitted, the timing, everything. They were talking about Rebecca's 'summer to forget' when she had by her own admission done a lot of things she would like to forget. It looked as if jumping into the bed of a formula-one champion driver had been one of them.

It was like seeing the last piece of a jigsaw slot horribly into place—she had always hated jigsaws.

Oh, God, Rebecca, how could you? Rose felt guilty for the selfish question the moment it popped into her head. If anyone had had a reason to go slightly off the rails that summer it had been her sister.

Simon with the floppy hair and the sweet smile had been the boy next door quite literally. He and Rebecca had been childhood sweethearts, dating since they were sixteen and engaged at nineteen.

Rose had been one of six bridesmaids—the wedding had *not* been a low-key affair—in a dress that had made her look almost slim. The sun had shone, the babies had refrained from crying, Rebecca had looked stunning like a dream bride.

The only thing missing had been the groom.

In response to a desperate phone call Rose had jumped in the vicar's Mini and gone to Simon's house. She had found the best man looking stunned in the driveway.

'Is it nerves?' she asked him.

He just looked at her, shook his head and asked for a cigarette. Rose reminded him he didn't smoke and went indoors. When she'd dragged the reason for his no show from the groom she briefly contemplated starting smoking herself.

'You have to tell her, Rose, I can't do it. Tell her I'm sorry and I love her, just not that way.'

'Oh, sure, that will make her feel much better. Shall I tell her before or after that her fiancé has waited until his wedding day to admit he's gay?' Rose wasn't in the mood to feel much empathy for anyone else but her twin that day.

Rose fully anticipated that Rebecca would collapse or lose it totally when she told her about Simon, but her sister was calm, almost surreally so considering the circumstances.

It was Rebecca who had taken control, which was good because their father was almost catatonic and their mother was stressing about the protocol of returning the gifts.

She insisted on telling the guests personally. Rose would never forget the image of her standing there like a serene goddess in her frothy white wedding dress explaining in a few dignified sentences that the wedding would not be going ahead.

Watching her, knowing how much she had to be hurting, broke Rose's heart; she knew that if the roles had been reversed she could never have been as brave.

It was about four days later that it actually hit Rebecca, then there were the tears, the anger…and a few weeks later she announced she had swung a refund on the honeymoon and some of the reception and planned to travel for a few months with the money.

It looked pretty much as if her travels had at some point taken her to Mathieu Gauthier's bedroom.

'It's gone quiet back there. Could it be your amnesia has been cured? Is it all coming back?' he suggested in a silky sneery voice that made Rose fantasise about wiping the superior smirk off his face.

'For your information…' She stopped the words playing in her mind—the tramp in your bed wasn't me, it was my twin sister.

It didn't matter how much she wanted to squeeze an apology out of the awful man. Her loyalty to her twin was more important. It was the very least that Rebecca deserved.

It wasn't as if it mattered one way or the other what Mathieu Demetrios or whatever he called himself these days thought of her.

She drew herself upright and, glaring at the back of his neck, shook her head, closing her mouth firmly on the retort. 'I've never been to Monaco.'

'Then you have a twin out there somewhere.'

Yes, I do, and I could give you her address, though I doubt her husband would be too happy about it. 'If you say so,' she agreed, shivering as she turned her head to look out of the window. 'I don't think the cottage hospital even has a casualty department.'

'It's a hospital. There will be a doctor.' If there wasn't it would have to be Inverness.

'I'm fine and I'm late…' She grabbed the door handle to steady herself as he took a corner clearly under the impression that he was still at the wheel of a formula-one car, not a battered Land Rover.

'We'll let the man who trained for six years decide if you're fine, shall we?'

Rose pursed her lips and didn't say another word. What was the point? He was clearly going to do what he wanted no matter what she said.

It turned out he was right, there was a doctor at the small community hospital—one of the local GPs who said they had done exactly the right thing when she related her story, apologising repeatedly for wasting his time.

When she returned to the waiting area a few minutes later she thought at first that her racing-driver rescuer had left…then just as some of the tension was leaving her spine he peeled himself away from a wall.

'Oh, I didn't see you in the shadow.' The tension was back with a vengeance. She had never met anyone who aroused such feelings of antipathy by doing nothing more than drawing himself up to his full and admittedly impressive height. It was lucky really—if she'd liked him she'd have felt that in some irrational way she was being disloyal to her twin.

'I said I'd wait.' His brows drew together in a straight line when she shivered.

'And I said it was not necessary. I'm quite capable of making my own way back.'

He arched a brow. 'Dressed like that.'

He had a point, she conceded, glancing down. The sweater covered as much as a dress, but it was a bit short and quite drafty. As for the man-sized woollen walking socks he'd dug out of the boot when she'd refused point-blank to allow him to carry her over the gravelled forecourt—well, they weren't exactly ideal footwear for public transport.

There was also the slight problem of her having no money.

She hated to be even more in his debt, but what choice did she have? 'I'm sorry to put you out. I'm sure you have more important things you should be doing.'

'Yes.'

Rose bit her lip. Clearly he was not into making people feel comfortable.

'Sorry,' she said again.

His lips quivered. The word was 'sorry' but the sentiment behind it was clearly 'go to hell'. His eyes slid to her feet encased in an old pair of Jamie's walking socks. To get there he had to move past her legs—they were very fine legs. They were the sort of legs a man could not look at without imagining himself between the soft, smooth thighs.

You passed, the voice in his head reminded him. It sounded disgusted and he could see why.

'What did the doctor say?' He found her more attractive in this weird get-up than he had that night in his hotel room. Did that, he wondered, make him twisted?

'He said what I said all along, I'm fine. He also said I was lucky.' She took a deep breath; not liking the man was no excuse for bad manners and he had risked his life to save her. 'And I am, thanks to you.'

He looked at the hand she had extended to him for a moment, then, just when she thought he was going to ignore it, he reached out and clasped it in his.

Rose's eyes flew wide and a small startled gasp escaped her parted lips before she could prevent it. She grunted something guarded and snatched her hand away. It was difficult to stay in denial about being wildly attracted to someone when you had a reaction like that to a simple handshake. She swallowed as she wondered about the electrical thrill that had shot through her body.

Did he feel it too?

She pushed aside the thought, ran her tongue over her dry lips and, still not looking at him, directed her words to the wall over his left shoulder. 'I really need to get back,' she said, her voice cracking with nerves.

He bowed his dark head slightly in acknowledgement of her request. 'Dornie House, you said…?' His eyes narrowed in concentration as he sketched a mental map of the area. If it was the place he thought he could stop by the estate and reassure Jamie that he hadn't dropped off the face of the earth.

'That's right.'

'The place off the Inverness road?'

'I think so.' She lifted a hand to her head.

As Mathieu watched the intensely weary gesture he was startled to feel his protective instincts stirring. He reminded himself who and what this woman was, but found it hard to reconcile the predatory man-eater of his memory with this exhausted and white-faced figure who had just narrowly escaped death…and there hadn't been a single tear.

You had to admire that. Whatever she was, she had guts.

'You walked a long way this morning. Come on.' She had to be tired because she didn't object when he placed a light guiding hand on her arm.

CHAPTER FIVE

'YOUR adrenaline levels are dropping,' Mathieu said, studying Rose's pale face with an expert eye. 'The delayed shock is kicking in,' he explained as he waited for her to swing her legs into the Land Rover before closing the passenger door. 'Are you sure the doctor said you were OK to leave?' he added when he slid into the driver's seat beside her.

You had to wonder about the competence of someone who sent a woman who looked ready to collapse home.

Rose nodded, but did not mention that the medic had only released her on the understanding she had someone to take care of her once she got home.

Home…it was ironic, after she had had such a fight to leave, that she had been suffering dreadfully from homesickness ever since she had arrived.

She knew it would pass, but at that moment she was feeling it particularly acutely. So acutely that she had to clamp her teeth into her lower lip to stop it trembling. The idea of showing that sort of weakness before this man horrified her.

'Have you moved here or are you visiting?'

With anyone else she would have suspected they were making conversation to give her time to compose herself. She lifted a hand to blot the moisture at the corner of one eye and sniffed. 'I'm working. I'm cataloguing Mr Smith's book collection.'

'*You're* cataloguing books?' He doubted she could have given a reply that would have surprised him more.

'Yes, when I'm not seducing men in their hotel rooms I'm a trained librarian.'

'Librarian?' He gave a sudden bark of laughter that brought a militant light to her amber eyes.

'What's so funny?'

He slid her a quick sideways glance. 'Well, you must admit it's not...well, a person doesn't look at you and think...' He turned his head again, the sweep of his eyes this time slow and sensual. Facing the road again, he grinned and shook his head. 'Well, he doesn't think librarian, *ma petite*.'

Why did French sound sexy even when a person was being sarcastic? And he must have been because nobody would call her his little one and be serious. 'You appear to have a very stereotypical image of a librarian, Mr Demetrios.' Did he make love in that language too?

Well, you're not going to find out, Rose, she told herself sternly. He threw Rebecca out of his bed and she's the size eight sexy one.

Was Rebecca right when she claimed being sexy was a state of mind? If she had meant thinking about sex, then that might well make me the sexiest person on the planet just now, Rose thought, embarrassed by her sudden preoccupation with the subject.

Meeting this man was going to put her in therapy.

'I won't ask what you think I look like.' Knowing what he thought she was was more than enough information.

'I try as a rule not to judge a book by its cover, but then you know all about books, don't you? You don't mind if I just swing by the estate to let Jamie know what's happened?' Without waiting for her response he took a sharp left. The entrance gates they passed through were grand but the tree-lined driveway beyond was potholed.

Rose had been here long enough to know that the estate, or Castle Clachan given its correct title, was occupied by the laird, a pretty important person hereabouts. She supposed it figured that someone like Mathieu would be on first-name terms with the man.

'You're staying here?'

He nodded and negotiated a particularly deep pothole. 'Jamie raced for a season.'

'Was he injured?'

'No, he just…you need…Jamie was a brilliant driver, but he lacked the…he wasn't, I suppose, ruthless enough. Jamie,' he explained, 'is much nicer than me.'

'An unnecessary explanation, I promise you.'

This drew a laugh from him. Rose couldn't help but notice what an attractive laugh he had.

They drew up on the gravelled area in front of the house. Well, actually there wasn't much gravel left, but there were a lot of weeds, though the house itself, a large sprawling Victorian pile in dressed stone, was impressive.

Mathieu seemed to read her thoughts. 'The original one dated to the fifteenth century; it burnt down, I believe. You wait here. I'll just let Jamie know…oh, there he is.'

Rose turned her head in time to see two men walk around the side of the house. One was tall, sandy-haired and, she assumed, the laird; the other was her employer. She began to struggle with the door handle. Now she knew why the car they had pulled up beside looked familiar.

Mathieu leaned across and caught her arm. 'What are you doing?'

'That's Mr Smith,' she said, drawing back into her seat as far as she could. 'I'm cataloguing his books.' Do not hyperventilate, Rose.

Mathieu turned his head. His mental image of Rose's

employer had made him a good twenty years older than the one talking to Jamie.

'You live in?'

Rose nodded, puzzled by the odd inflection in his voice, but relieved she was no longer pressed into her seat by his arm. It didn't even cross her mind that Mathieu might be wondering about the sleeping arrangements and if she had guessed she would have laughed. Robert Smith, despite the fact he was youngish and quite good-looking, was peculiarly sexless and a humourless cold fish to boot.

'You stay there. I'll explain what's happened.'

Jamie greeted him with his usual hearty good humour. Though his expression sobered when Mathieu explained what had happened.

'Lucky you were around, old mate.'

'Yes, most fortunate,' Robert Smith agreed. 'But you say that Miss Hall is not hurt—the doctor gave her a clean bill of health?'

'She's shaken, obviously.'

'I'm sure once she's working she'll forget all about it.'

'Working?'

The other man flushed under the sardonic stare. 'Well, I thought…I have a schedule and—'

'She needs to rest.'

Robert Smith visibly recoiled from the blaze of fury in the other man's eyes. 'Oh, well, if that's what the doctor recommends, of course I'll make sure she—'

'Robert,' Jamie drawled, clapping the man on the back. 'Why don't you just toddle along in and look at those books? I left them on the hall table.'

The other man accepted the invitation with alacrity.

'I'll just go and speak to Miss Hall first.'

'I think you scared him,' Jamie said in an amused undertone as the other man began to walk towards the Land Rover.

'I think the man,' Mathieu said scornfully, 'is an idiot.'

'Yes, that came across,' Jamie said drily. 'Rich, though—made a bomb in the City and retired young. I thought I might sell off a few old books, seems he's mad about them. So the girl…do I get an introduction?' He glanced curiously towards the Land Rover. 'Why don't I ever get the opportunity to play the white knight to damsels in distress?' he complained.

Mathieu's glance followed the direction of Jamie's stare. Rose, presumably at the suggestion of Smith, was getting out of the Land Rover. His brow furrowed as she nodded at the other man and began to walk towards them. 'She's changed a lot…since Monaco.'

Mathieu wasn't even aware he had verbalised his thoughts until Jamie spoke.

'You know her! My God, what are the odds on that?' Jamie, his eyes widening in appreciation, gave a low whistle under his breath as Rose got closer. 'Any chance of an intro, Matt?'

Mathieu flashed Jamie an irritated look. 'I hardly know her…we met—' he began, then stopped as Rose came within hearing distance. She stood there looking, despite her outlandish outfit and gloriously tousled hair, dignified and beautiful enough to offer some excuse for Jamie's childish outburst.

'Hello.' Rose nodded towards Jamie, her smile dimming perceptively as her eyes reached Mathieu. 'Mr Smith is giving me a lift back. I just wanted to thank you…again…for, well, saving my life,' she said awkwardly. 'And I'm sorry for putting you to so much trouble.'

'Saving your life?' Jamie interrupted, stepping forward, hand outstretched, to introduce himself. 'Played that part down, Matt.' He flashed his friend an amused sideways glance. 'But then that's our Matt all over, the modest hero.'

The modest hero in question looked uncomfortable and irritated and his grin broadened. 'We've not met, though in a place this size it was only a matter of time. I'm Jamie.'

'I know—the laird.'

'For the present, but I'm hoping Matt here will do something brilliant and keep the bailiffs from the door.'

Rose found it hard to tell from his tone if he was joking or not, but what did come across was his confidence in Mathieu's ability to pull off the odd miracle in his spare time. She found herself hoping that on this occasion Mathieu did so because it was hard not to warm to the young laird.

'I'm Rose. If you'll excuse me—' she glanced expressively down at her clothes before extricating her hand and wrapping her arms around herself '—I'll just go wait in the car. It's warmer.' Rose smiled once more before turning away.

'I think she likes me,' Jamie said under his breath as she walked back to the parked vehicle. 'No so sure about you, though.'

'So what books are you selling?'

It seemed for a moment that his change of subject might work, but, mid-description of a book, Jamie stopped and angled a sharp look at his friend. *'Monaco…'*

Mathieu shrugged and pretended ignorance.

'You said you knew her in Monaco.'

'It might have been.'

'My God, it's her, isn't it? The blonde that got into your room the night of the embassy party.'

Mathieu, his expression schooled to neutrality, held his tongue, though he suspected rather too late in the day.

'I take it that silence means yes.' Jamie let out a long silent whistle followed by a cackle of laughter. 'Someone who works for Smith doesn't seem the type…she didn't seem the type. Though, to be honest,' he admitted rather regretfully, 'I've not had a whole lot of experience of the sort of women who try and seduce men they've never met. Was she totally naked?'

Mathieu flashed him a flat look.

Jamie held up a pacifying hand. 'All right, no need to implode.

You sure nothing happened? I mean, was there a frisson out there on the ice?' Grinning, he raised a speculative brow.

Mathieu did not smile back. 'You have an overactive imagination, Jamie,' he said coolly.

This time Jamie did read the warning in the other man's manner. 'If you say so…' he said in his easygoing way. 'But I suppose you do know, Mathieu, that you're one of the few men in the universe who would get mad about finding a naked beautiful blonde in his bed.'

'I don't like surprises, I suppose.' His dark brows drew into a straight line above his hawkish nose. 'I don't know why I ever told you about it,' he added, the exasperation in his voice aimed mostly at himself.

'You didn't have much choice after I heard you lambasting the hotel staff on their security,' Jamie reminded him. 'Weren't you even slightly tempted to take what was on offer? I mean, the delicious Rose is pretty hot…' His wistful sigh was accompanied by a lecherous grin.

It was a grin that Mathieu had a problem with.

His long fingers tightened until his knuckles turned white. His dark lashes came down in a veil as he took a deep breath that did little to reduce the angry pounding in his temples.

'Do people here have nothing better to do than gossip?' he asked coldly.

'Not really,' Jamie admitted. Then, oblivious to the fact his friend was fighting violent urges, he continued to speculate about the blonde.

'I wonder if she'd like to come and catalogue my book collection after she finishes with Smith?' His comic suggestive leer faded dramatically in the face of the flash of livid fury on his friend's face.

It was at that moment that Robert Smith announced his presence by clearing his throat.

Both men turned in unison.

'I'm afraid, James, that the books…well, they're not quite what I'm looking for.'

Jamie took the news with a philosophical shrug. 'Oh, well, not to worry.'

'I have a friend who might be interested and I'll mention them to him if you like? I'm afraid, though, they're really not that valuable.'

'I'll buy them,' Mathieu heard himself say.

Jamie looked as surprised by the offer as Mathieu felt. 'You don't know what they are,' he pointed out.

'I have a bookshelf to fill.'

'Right, then, I'll be off.'

Mathieu's lip curled into a contemptuous smile. 'The schedule?' he suggested.

The other man struggled to smile back. 'Just so…and thank you once more for helping Miss Hall.'

Mathieu watched, his eyes narrowed, as Smith got into the car beside Rose. 'I don't like that man.'

Jamie fought a grin. 'And you hid it so well, Matt,' he said, clapping a congratulatory hand on his friend's arm. 'As you're on a roll with the saving-people thing…about my finances—is it hopeless?'

Seeing the real concern behind his friend's levity, Mathieu dragged his thoughts from the unlikely librarian and back to his friend's financial situation.

CHAPTER SIX

ALL the way over in the taxi Rose kept going over the morning's scene in her head.

'I'm afraid, Miss Hall, that I must let you go.'

Jaw clenched, Rose turned her head and stared out of the window not seeing the stunning Highland scenery, dusted that morning by a sprinkling of snow. She squeezed her eyes tight and shook her head. She hadn't had an inkling of what was to come even after that opening, but then she hadn't woken up expecting to receive her marching orders.

'Let me go?'

'I no longer think we can work together.'

'You're giving me the sack?' She was too astonished to be angry…that presumably would come later—*and it had*. 'But I don't understand. The job is only half done. Have you some complaint about my work? Is this because I spent the rest of the day in bed yesterday, because I would have worked if—'

'Your work has been adequate,' Robert Smith conceded stiffly. 'However, certain other matters have been brought to my attention.'

'What matters?'

He started moving objects around his desk, not quite meeting her eyes. 'I have given the matter some thought since yesterday.' He gave a sigh and lifted his head. 'And unfortunately I have concluded it would be quite unsuitable for a woman of your...' He stopped, clearing his throat.

'A woman of my what?'

Lips pursed, his eyes cold behind the horn-rimmed glasses as they slid from hers, he said, 'This is a small community; there are no secrets. Your exploits, Rose, will soon be common knowledge.'

'Exploits?' Rose echoed, still in the dark.

'The people here are old-fashioned and as an incomer I have to respect their values. I did have some concern initially about having such a young woman living here,' he admitted, and Rose thought, God, does every man I meet think I'm out to ravish him? 'But as you are well qualified I put my concerns to one side. Now, of course, that is out of the question given your dubious history...'

Rose laughed. She couldn't help herself, the idea was so ludicrous. Then it hit her in a blinding flash. Her eyes narrowing, she asked in a dangerously calm voice, 'Have you been talking to Mathieu Demetrios?' So much for 'your secret is safe with me'— he hadn't been able to wait five minutes to spread his vile lies.

The worm! Not content with humiliating her personally, he had set out with what had to be deliberate malice to ruin her reputation, or, as it happened, Rebecca's. What a sly, vindictive bastard. If she had ever needed confirmation on her decision not to reveal the case of mistaken identity, she had it.

All she stood to lose was her job and she had.

'Of course, I will pay you until the end of the month.'

She would have been the first to advise anyone who found themselves in a similar situation to maintain a dignified silence, take the money that she was due and put the entire episode down to experience.

It was excellent advice, but Rose had found herself unable to refrain from telling her erstwhile employer that she wouldn't touch his money with a bargepole, and he wasn't likely to repeat the offer—not after she had been pretty frank when she had offered her opinion of him.

Rose asked the driver to wait, which was probably reckless considering her financial situation, but when she made her big exit she didn't want to have it fall flat because she had to beg a lift to the station.

It was not a uniformed flunky who opened the vast oak-studded door, but Jamie MacGregor's sister home for the school holiday. Her look of shock when she saw Rose morphed into a wary smile.

'Oh, hi. I saw you yesterday. You might not have seen me,' she added awkwardly.

Rose was too preoccupied to wonder at the teenager's odd manner. 'No, I didn't.'

'You work for Mr Smith.'

'Not any more.'

'Do you want Jamie?'

'I want Mathieu.'

The young girl registered Rose's gritted teeth, angry eyes and flushed teeth and gave a nervous giggle.

'I'm afraid…the thing is I don't think that…'

Rose cut across her. 'I don't give a damn if he's busy or unavailable or anything else because I intend to see him whether he wants to see me or not.'

'I, really, they're—'

'I want Mathieu.'

'I am quite naturally flattered.'

'You shouldn't be,' Rose snapped, tilting her head up to a combative angle to glare at the tall figure that had materialised at the girl's shoulder.

She blinked as her gaze travelled up from his gleaming

handmade leather shoes to his glossy head. This was the first time she had seen him dressed in anything so formal as a suit and tie. And not just any suit. She was no expert, but it was obvious even to Rose that the dark grey single-breasted number was no more off the peg than the body it covered, and she had to admit Mathieu looked nothing short of breathtakingly spectacular in it.

Some men relied on power suits to give them presence. Mathieu didn't need to; he had more presence than any man ought to be allowed.

Enough presence to make her slightly dizzy when she stared at him.

Then don't stare.

Damned good recommendation, but not one Rose could observe. It would have been nice, she thought wistfully, to find something…one tiny flaw she could criticise.

But there was none.

He looked tall and impressive, the discreet tailoring of the dark, beautifully cut jacket emphasising the powerful breadth of his shoulders. It hung open revealing a crisp white shirt made of a fabric fine enough to show a faint shadow of the body hair on his chest, sending her stomach into a lurching dive.

'What are you doing lurking like that?' Her nerves found release in snapping antagonism.

He arched one brow sardonically. He loosened his tie and allowed his eyes—actually, it was not something over which he had much control—to wander over her soft feminine curves before explaining. 'I'm on my way to Edinburgh.'

There were occasions when being a Demetrios had its advantages, and he had the financial clout that went with the name to arrange a meeting at a few hours' notice with the bank that was threatening to pull the plug on Jamie and the ailing estate.

The phone calls had gone pretty much as he had anticipated. The money men had been negative initially. They'd liked his plan, called it innovative and daring, but the bottom line, they had explained, was it was too late in the day.

'Of course, Mr Demetrios, if someone else was willing to invest…share the risk the bank has already taken…?'

That too had been a response Mathieu had anticipated. He had made only one stipulation. Jamie, he had explained to them, must never know who his new investor was.

Mathieu looked thoughtfully down at the flushed angry face of his visitor and bent his head. 'Fiona, I think Jamie was looking for you,' he said without taking his eyes off Rose.

With a show of reluctance and several curious looks the young girl left them.

'Can I come in or should I go around to the tradesmen's entrance?'

He bowed slightly from the waist and stepped back for her to enter the hallway. 'I think, yes,' he said, pushing open one of the heavy doors that led off the vaulted hallway, 'we can be private in here.'

'Oh, very big on confidentiality all of a sudden, aren't we?' she muttered, following him inside the room.

She vaguely registered the oak-panelled walls, and the obligatory stag's head on the wall, but her attention was concentrated on the figure who preceded her.

Nothing she could say was likely to make him feel guilty; wrecking lives was probably one of the highlights of his day.

She watched as he bent to throw a log from the stack beside the vast stone fireplace on the fire that brightened the gloomy room.

The log crackled into fiery life. So did her temper when he turned around, set his shoulders to the jutting stone mantle and said politely, 'Is there something I can help you with, Rose?'

'You could drop dead.' She clamped her lips to prevent any further childish retorts that gave him the opportunity to look down at her in that superior way from escaping.

'How things change,' he bemoaned, his eyes glimmering mockery as he casually pulled the tie from around his neck. 'And I thought you were different, Rose.'

Rose dragged her eyes from the small vee of brown skin revealed at his throat as he slipped the top button of his shirt and glared up at him with renewed venom.

'Once you liked me a good deal better, but a man learns who his real friends are when he leaves behind the glamour of the racing circuit.'

'I'm sure you still have an entourage of hangers-on and people willing to treat your every stupid pronouncement as wise and wonderful. Men like you always do.'

'Have you known a lot of men like me?'

'No, I've been lucky that way, though if I saw any coming I'd cross to the other side of the street.'

He pursed his lips and loosed a long silent whistle. 'Someone got out of bed the wrong side this morning.'

'This morning I had a bed.'

He levered himself off the stone mantle and took a step towards her. 'And you don't now?'

'No, I don't. No bed, no job.'

'You quit?'

'No, I was sacked.'

'Smith sacked you.' He shook his head, his expression one of mild contempt as he thought of the other man. 'I didn't see that one coming.' That certainly explained her mood, but not her presence.

The rueful amusement in his expression made her see red. 'Liar!'

He froze, the lines of his lean face moulding into a mask of chilling hauteur. 'What did you call me?'

Rose lifted her chin to a belligerent angle and placed her hands on her hips. She had no intention of allowing herself to be intimidated, even though he did have the look of a jungle predator about to pounce.

'You heard me.' She lifted her chin and ignored the sound of hissing outrage that escaped through his clenched white teeth. 'You're many things, but you're not stupid.'

'Thank you,' he said, his voice dripping with mockery.

'You must have thought of the consequences when you told everyone I'm a drunken nymphomaniac?'

'I did not tell anyone anything of the sort…' He stopped, an expression of pained comprehension passing across his face as he slapped a hand to his forehead and swore.

Rose's head came up with a jerk. 'Well, it's the sort of thing that could slip anyone's mind, I suppose.'

He bit back a cutting response to her sarcasm and watched, his expression softening, as she rubbed a hand wearily across her eyes with the back of her hand.

'I hope, incidentally, that it makes an amusing after-dinner anecdote.'

'I can't believe he actually sacked you.' He regarded her with frowning concern.

'And I can't believe you actually care,' she cut back. 'But I really don't see why the concept is so hard to get your head around. What did you expect my boss to do when you told him I was a groupie—give me a raise?' Her lip wobbled and a tear escaped from the corner of her eye. 'Damn,' she muttered, brushing it away. 'Why does this happen when I'm mad?' Her head dropped as she fought to regain her composure.

As he studied her bent head and watched her hunched slender shoulders shake Mathieu experienced an alien and compelling urge to take her in his arms. It was followed by an almost equally violent need to throttle her idiot employer.

'I did not relate the story.' He half expected her to resist when he put a hand in the narrow of her back and steered her towards the nearest chair, but she didn't. 'Sit down before you fall down.' Impatience masked the concern he didn't want to be feeling.

Why should he feel responsible? It was not his fault that she had worked for someone who was parochial and intolerant. Neither, despite what she thought, had he been telling tales.

'I did not relay the story at all. I suppose it's possible he simply overheard something that Jamie said.' Mathieu looked doubtful.

'*Jamie…?*' Brushing her hair from her face with her forearm, Rose tilted her head and looked up at him, rolling her eyes in disbelief. 'My God, is there anyone you didn't tell?'

'Jamie was in the hotel that night. He heard me complaining about the hotel security and he wormed the story out of me. When he saw you he guessed…'

'Guessed,' she echoed. 'You must have dropped some pretty heavy clues.'

'I didn't need to. Jamie doesn't miss much. If it's any comfort, as a consequence of seeing you my standing in his eyes has plummeted.'

With a dry laugh she lifted her head. 'That I doubt.'

'It was me, I think.'

Both turned in unison as the door swung inwards to reveal Fiona standing there. Jamie's sister looked the picture of guilt.

Mathieu's brows twitched into a straight line of disapproval. 'Fiona, have you been eavesdropping?'

'Yes…no, that is, it wasn't deliberate the *other* time.'

Mathieu's brows lifted. 'Other time?'

Fiona's eyes slid from his as she shuffled her feet miserably and mumbled, 'I heard you and Jamie talking about Monaco and the hotel and…' her eyes lifted to Rose '…you. Grace said—'

'*Grace?*' Mathieu ran a hand along his jaw, looking impatient. 'Who is Grace?'

'Who is Grace?' Fiona echoed, sounding indignant. 'You know who she is. She's been my best friend for ever, or since we were four anyway…her dad runs the climbing centre. I texted her and, well, she might have texted Ellie and Ellie probably sent an email to a few other people.'

'Oh, my God,' Rose breathed shakily. 'I think the mystery of how Mr Smith knows the story is solved,' she said in a shaky voice. 'The only mystery is how there's anybody left this side of Inverness who doesn't know.' Hearing the note of hysteria in her voice, she bit her lip.

Presumably Mathieu heard it too, because he looked at her oddly before he jerked his head at the teenager and snapped, 'Out.' A tearful Fiona fled and he walked across to a bureau, out of which he produced a bottle and a glass. 'Jamie's best malt,' he said, filling the glass.

'If that's for me,' Rose said, shaking her head as he walked towards her, 'I don't like whisky.'

'It's medicinal,' he said, handing it to her.

With a sigh of irritation she took the glass. 'I've lost my job. I'm angry, not ill.'

'It's true, you know. Take a sip, it'll steady your nerves.'

Not while you're standing this close, she thought, lifting the liquid to her lips. 'What's true?' she asked, giving a shudder at the taste the sip of peaty malt left in her mouth.

'It's true Jamie thinks that any man who threw you out of his bed needs therapy.' Maybe he was right, Mathieu thought as his eyes were drawn once more to the soft lush outline of her pink lips.

'I wouldn't mind,' she mused, staring into the bottom of the glass, 'if I had actually done anything…no, actually, I would mind,' she burst out, levelling a burning resentful glare at Mathieu. 'So long as I did my job well, my personal life is none of his business, the narrow-minded, pompous little bigot. He said people might get the wrong idea about our relationship. Can you imagine?' she asked, her voice rising in an incredulous note, before she added with a bitter laugh, 'Sleep with that cold fish. God,' she muttered, 'I'd rather sleep with *you*!'

'I'm flattered.'

Rose put down the glass very carefully. This interview was not going as planned; by now she ought to be making a grand sweeping exit. The alcohol and fire, she decided, were having an undesirable mellowing effect.

'Don't be,' she advised. 'If there's one thing I despise more than a sanctimonious prig, it's a man who can't resist boasting about his conquests to the boys.'

'*Conquest?*' His dark brows rose. 'Your memory of the occasion is no doubt hazy, but we didn't actually—'

'No, because I wasn't good enough for you!' Almost before the words were out of her mouth Rose was struck by the incongruity of her reaction to his jibe.

While she felt indignant about the rejection on her twin's behalf, she also felt relieved. Relieved that Mathieu had resisted Rebecca's advances, because if he hadn't... Her thoughts skittered to a halt as a look of stupefied shock spread across her face.

I'd have been jealous!

She skimmed a look up at the man responsible for this foreign emotion. She had never been jealous of her twin even though there had been ample cause. Rebecca was always the talented one, the slim one, the passionate one. The one that men were drawn to.

But Mathieu hadn't been.

'You were drunk.' Mathieu dragged his eyes from the heaving contours of her bosom at that moment outlined in heather-blue angora.

'It wasn't me,' she snarled through gritted teeth. 'How many times do I have to tell you? My God, but you are so judgemental. Haven't you ever done anything you regret?'

'I suppose it is something that you can regret it.'

'Did it ever occur to you that there might be a reason for her behaviour? A reason that had nothing to do with you being totally irresistible for what she did that night? Did it ever occur to you that she might have been going through a really traumatic time in her life? That she might have found out the man she was engaged to, the man who dumped her at the altar, was gay?'

Mathieu watched as she stopped to catch her breath. Presumably her use of the third person was part of the denial thing she had going on.

'You were engaged to be married?' There was an inflection in his deep voice that she couldn't quite pin down, but Rose immediately knew that she had made a tactical error.

Her instinctive desire to offer an explanation for Rebecca's uncharacteristic behaviour had only resulted in him believing she was trying to excuse herself.

Eyes shut tight, she groaned in sheer frustration as she bellowed, 'Not me; we are not talking about me.'

Mathieu, it seemed, was.

'Of course not.'

This was said with such obvious insincerity that she wanted to scream.

Mathieu looked down at his hands and saw they were bunched into fists at his sides. It was irrational to feel the sort of violent antagonism he was experiencing for a total stranger. He took a deep breath and forced his tensed muscles to relax.

'Who was he?'

'Look, I really don't want to discuss my personal life with you.'

'At least you now admit it is your personal life.'

Rose rolled her eyes in frustration. What was the point denying it when he obviously wasn't going to listen?

'I can see that it must have been a shock, but I'm sure you will agree in retrospect that getting drunk and sleeping with strangers was not the wisest response,' he continued.

'You have obviously never been in love.' She studied his lean face with dislike, and thought it was a safe bet that there had been droves of women who fancied themselves in love with him.

Blinded by his exotic heritage, dark devastating looks and charismatic smile, not to mention the raw sex appeal he exuded from every pore.

'You feel equipped to make this assumption because…?'

Rose blinked. 'You've been dumped?' She gave a laugh of total incredulity as her glance travelled up the long, lean length of him. 'Now that I don't believe.'

His lips twitched and a gleam that she deeply distrusted entered his dark eyes. 'It might be that not everybody finds me as irresistible as you do.'

'For a man with power, position and money a lot of women would be willing to overlook a good many flaws.'

'You are not very charitable to your sisters.'

'I doubt if I have anything in common with your lovers.' Thinking of them did not improve her mood. 'You know, it would serve you right if I went around telling everyone that you were awful in bed…' If she had a reputation she might as well use it.

Rose was startled when her threat drew what seemed like a totally genuine laugh from him…genuine and attractive, she thought, very conscious of the butterfly-wings sensation low in her belly. It was the brandy on an empty stomach, she told herself.

'You think I'm joking?' she asked him belligerently. 'I would, you know.'

He shook his head. 'No, I'm sure you would. The only problem is I think you're assuming I have a fragile male ego. I don't. I imagine,' he mused, not smiling, 'it is partly to do with genetics and—'

'And partly,' she cut in contemptuously, 'to do with every woman in your life telling you how perfect you are.' Poor deluded idiots. 'Newsflash, Mathieu, women lie.'

'You being the exception.'

'Well, I'm not about to tell you you're perfect,' she promised grimly as she rose to her feet with slightly wobbly dignity. 'I've said what I came to, I'm going now and I just…no.' She broke off and lifted her blazing eyes to his before placing her shoulder bag very firmly on top of her case beside the chair. 'I'm not going anywhere.' No way, that would be letting him off too easily.

She had come here to vent her feelings and hopefully prick his conscience, but she could see now that it had been naïve of her to expect him to exhibit some remorse. The man was a total stranger to compassion.

'You messed up my life—you can put it right.'

The smile was wiped from his face. A spasm of distaste contorted the perfectly proportioned contours of his lean features. 'And how much will this putting right cost me?'

'Cost?' She stared up at him in bewilderment. Then as his meaning sank in the colour left her cheeks as a wave of revolted fury washed over her. This hateful man couldn't open his mouth without insulting her.

'You think I'm asking you for cash? I wouldn't take money off you if I were dead,' she declared in a quivering voice.

He looked down at her for a moment, his expression considering. 'If that were the situation money wouldn't do you much good, but as you are very much alive…' His eyes moved from the sparkling scorn in her bright eyes, and touched the soft fullness of her lips before sliding slowly across the smooth opalescent skin of her slender throat.

'I don't want your money; I want a job,' she declared.

He looked perplexed by her explanation. 'A job?'

CHAPTER SEVEN

'YES, I want a job, the thing I had until you decided to slander me to anyone that would listen.'

'I haven't slandered you to anyone, I told you—'

Rose cut off his weary explanation with a bored wave of her hand. 'Yeah, yeah… It seems to me that under the circumstances it's the least you could do.'

'Slander is a crime.'

Rose shrugged, lowered her eyes from his lean face and thought looking sinfully seductive and dangerous ought to be one too.

'And I'm sure you have a team of lawyers who make damned sure that nothing you don't like ever gets said or printed about you.'

'That might not be such a bad idea,' he conceded.

'Are you laughing at me?' she asked, studying his solemn expression suspiciously.

He took a step closer and looked at her with his dark head inclined to one side. The expression she didn't trust was still in his eyes, but she was no longer sure it was laughter. Whatever it was it made her heart beat a lot faster against her breastbone.

'You could sue me,' he suggested softly.

Rose held her ground even though every instinct she had was screaming at her to run. The charge that he gave off was electrical, almost physical; her own reaction was definitely physical. Just being this close to him made her toes tingle and her stomach quiver.

'And don't think I wouldn't if it wasn't for…' She stopped, biting her lip.

'If it wasn't for what?'

Rose dropped her eyes and shook her head. 'Just thank your lucky stars I'm not litigious,' she gritted back huskily. 'The legal system is loaded in favour of people like you, anyway.' Even as she said it Rose knew the stereotyping was flawed; this man might be despicable, but he was not part of the herd. He was unique.

'Like me?'

His dangerously low-voiced query made Rose wind her anger around her like a protective scarf. 'You know, if you possessed a fraction of the moral fibre you like to shove down other people's throats,' she yelled, 'you'd own up to the fact it was your fault I lost my job and want to put it right.'

Mathieu watched as she sucked in a wrathful breath causing a good deal of quivering under the soft angora. The blazing gold eyes that meshed with his were shimmering with tears of anger. 'Want…?' he echoed thickly and swallowed.

The truth was at that precise moment the only thing that he wanted to do was drag her into his arms and kiss her senseless. The raw, primitive nature of the response she drew from him was like nothing he had ever experienced before.

He had had the opportunity to do a lot more than kiss her and he had walked away. When offered on a plate what his body now craved, he had been able to reject it with no difficulty.

What had changed?

Four years ago he had been aesthetically aware of the beauty of the woman who had offered herself to him, but he had not been tempted. There had been no chemistry.

Yet now he could not be in the same room as her, or even think of the scent of her perfume, without feeling the stirring of desire.

A bemused groove between his darkly defined brows, his brooding glance drifted speculatively across the soft contours of her face. Emotional and physical control was something he pretty much took for granted, he was master of his appetites and he had met women who were more beautiful, so what was it about this one, beyond the obvious, that ate away at his discipline? And why now and not four years earlier?

'But, of course, someone like you wouldn't understand what it is like to lose a job.'

He arched a dark brow as he met her scornful glare. 'What exactly am I like, Rose?' He liked the way her name felt on his tongue; it led him to wondering how she would taste.

'I'd tell you if I thought it would do any good, but no matter what I say you'll still carry on thinking you're God's gift to the human race and the female part of it in particular.' Her angry gaze grew distracted as it stilled on his lean dark face. Wouldn't anyone who looked in the mirror and saw that face every morning be arrogant?

'But basically you're someone who wouldn't have a clue what it means to lose a job. We don't all have a private income to fall back on.'

'You have a family to go home to—you won't exactly starve.'

'I have a family and I have savings, but that's not the point. I'm twenty-six. I don't want to sponge off my parents.' And neither did she want to go back and have everyone say *I told you so*.

'You assume that I have led a rich, pampered existence?' Anything less pampered than his life up to the age of fifteen would have been difficult to imagine.

Yet in many ways those years when there had been just himself and his mother living what many would consider a deprived, hand-to-mouth existence had been in the ways that counted the happiest of his life.

Mathieu was in a position to know firsthand that money and

material possessions did not buy happiness. He had wanted for nothing materially when Andreos had recognised him as his son. But that first year there had been many occasions when if someone had offered him the chance to return to the life he had had before Andreos he would have taken it without a second thought.

Rose felt a rush of anger. Surely he wouldn't be hypocritical enough to suggest anything else. 'Now why should I assume that when you're standing there in your fancy suit and handmade Italian shoes?' she drawled sarcastically. 'I suppose you've spent no end of nights worrying about paying bills.'

'Not lost sleep,' he conceded. 'But I have needed to—what is the expression? Rob Peter to pay Paul.'

Suspecting his mockery, she glared. 'Oh, yes, I'm sure you had it tough.'

A flicker of sardonic amusement flashed into his eyes as he lifted his shoulders in a minimal but expressive shrug. 'You might be surprised.'

Rose looked at him in disgust and he looked back with a faint smile and cool confidence that went bone-deep. Was that confidence a result of his privileged upbringing or was that inherent in the man?

Rose suspected the latter was true.

'Surprised that a man who is wearing a watch that costs more than some houses knows what it's like to be hard up,' she tossed at him scornfully and folded her arms across her chest. 'Frankly, yes, I would be surprised. Very surprised. You're heir to a huge fortune…squillions!'

And even if his wealth hadn't been common knowledge it would be obvious just by looking at him, she reflected, her gaze travelling up the long, lean, supremely elegant length of him, that he was part of an exclusive élite.

'I wouldn't be surprised if your silver spoon was encrusted with diamonds,' she speculated bitterly. 'What's so funny?' she demanded indignantly in response to his dry laugh.

The satirical glitter faded from Mathieu's eyes, leaving his expression sombre as he said, 'I didn't always have a silver spoon, Rose.'

She slung him an irritated glare and swung away, or she would have if he hadn't caught her by the shoulder and twisted her back.

'Do you mind?' Her breath was coming in painful little gasps as she forced her eyes away from the disturbing image of his brown fingers curled over her upper arm. 'I don't enjoy this hands-on stuff,' she claimed, even though her entire treacherous body was doing its best to reveal her as a liar.

She mentally crossed her fingers and hoped he would put down the tremors that were rippling through her body to her revulsion. Fortunately there was no way he could know anything about the warm, squidgy, fluttery feeling low in her belly. And unless she fell down in a heap the weakened state of her knees would remain on a strictly need-to-know basis.

Even so she half expected Mathieu to respond with a scornful laugh, but he didn't. As their eyes connected she stopped struggling.

'Mathieu…?'

'I was born in a single-roomed apartment in an area of Paris that the tourists do not visit.'

Rose stared. The words that had literally shocked her into silence had erupted from his lips with an intensity that made her take an involuntary step backwards. In the split second before she saw his smooth urbane mask slide into place she saw a flicker of shock in his eyes. It was almost as if he was as surprised as she was to hear what he said.

'Actually nobody visits there unless they have no other choice.' His taut smile did not reach his eyes and his previous stark announcement hung in the air between them. 'But that is not relevant.' The words, his manner—they both signalled his intention to draw a line under the subject. A subject you introduced, Matt.

'But I don't understand.'

Mathieu's jaw tightened. Neither did he. He didn't understand what impulse had made him volunteer personal information that way. He might as well have handed the woman a gold-edged invite to tramp around in his head.

It was bizarre. Andreos had said a lot worse and utterly failed to get under his guard, but for some reason Rose's silver-spoon jibe, not to mention her assumption of moral superiority when she had made it, had really got to him.

Since when did he give a damn what anyone thought of him? It didn't matter to him if Rose Hall dismissed him as some spoilt, pampered rich kid who had grown into a spoilt, pampered man.

'What are you talking about?'

His lashes lifted from his chiselled cheekbones. 'I'm not.'

'You can't say something like that and leave it,' she protested.

He gave a very Gallic shrug. 'Why not?'

Rose rolled her eyes. 'Are you serious?'

'I am not the subject of this conversation.' His sanity possibly should be. For the first time in his life he was worried that if he started talking he couldn't guarantee where the cut-off point would be. He had already let this woman have a glimpse of himself that should have remained private. That was a pretty heavy price to pay just for the pleasure of the look of smug superiority wiped off her face.

'Your father is Andreos Demetrios, isn't he?' Just about the richest man in Europe and Mathieu was his heir. How could what he was saying be true?

A growling sound escaped Mathieu's clamped lips as he bared his teeth in a ferocious smile and glared down at her. She was like a damned terrier with a bone.

Rose, who didn't have a clue what she had done to earn such seething resentment, kept her chin up but regarded him warily.

'You want the salacious details? Fine.' His lip curled contemptuously as he punched the air in a gesture of frustration and asked himself, 'Why not?' before dragging a hand through his hair. 'Andreos is my father; I have the DNA results to prove it. But my mother,' he continued in the same driven manner, 'was not his wife. My mother was a young girl who gave birth nine months after a one-night stand.'

'Then you were a…'

'A bastard—yes, I am.' Her embarrassed flush brought his mocking smile to the surface.

'And you had no contact with him…your father…when you were young?' A pucker appeared on her smooth brow. 'Surely he gave your mother financial support.'

'It was only after my mother's death that I learned who my father was.'

'Didn't you ask? Weren't you curious?' It seemed inconceivable to Rose that anyone would not want to know their roots.

He shook his dark head, his expression remote as though his thoughts were in another time and place. 'We were fine as we were, just the two of us.'

'Did he know?'

'About me? Apparently not. I went to live with him six months after she died.' He related the information in a flat, expressionless tone…well, having revealed this much there seemed very little point holding back now. *Dieu*, what was it about this woman that activated some previously dormant soul-bearing gene in his make-up?

She met his eyes. All she could see was her own reflection in the mirrored silver surface. His expression, in stark contrast to the blaze of white-hot emotion that had been written there moments earlier, was inscrutable. 'It is sad, your mother being alone…'

'She wasn't alone; she had me.'

'How old were you when she died?'

'Nearly fifteen.'

'And that six months before you went to live with him?'

Mathieu ran a hand over his jaw and nodded. It was years since he had even allowed himself to think about that time in his life. There was something almost liberating about allowing himself to share these private recollections.

'I stayed on in the flat and I worked as a construction labourer to pay the rent.' These were things he had never told anyone—not even Jamie, his best friend.

'But you were fifteen,' Rose exclaimed, her eyes round with shock.

'I was tall for my age.'

'That's not what I meant. You were a child—you shouldn't have been alone that way. You should have been at school.'

'I didn't go to school when she got ill, and afterwards...' He gave a careless shrug. 'I suppose I fell through the cracks. Look,' he said, changing the subject abruptly, 'whether you believe it or not, I am sorry you lost your job, but I have no vacancy that would suit your qualifications.'

'I'm a qualified librarian, but I haven't always worked with books.' As she looked at him Rose was unable to shake the image from her head of him as a lonely little boy forced first to care for his dying mother and then to fend for himself. Her tender heart ached when she thought about it.

'I know what you're good at,' he said, his eyes lingering on her lush mouth as he once again was overwhelmed with the urge to kiss it, 'and that I can get it for free.'

Mathieu moved his head to one side just a split second before her hand would have connected with his cheek. He caught her wrist and surprised her almost as much as he did himself by bringing it up to his mouth and brushing the smooth blue-veined inner aspect of her wrist with his lips.

Eyes wide, she released a small cry and pulled back. Mathieu released his hold and watched as she nursed her hand against her heaving breasts.

'Sorry, that was a cheap crack.' And he had made it to drive the look of compassion from her face… If there was one thing he could not tolerate, it was pity.

Rose's head came up; he had sounded genuinely regretful.

'And not true,' he continued. 'Nothing is for free in this world.'

This cynical outlook caused her brow to furrow, but she bit back her instinctive protest.

'We all of us do things we regret in life. It is not helpful to be reminded of them constantly, especially when you have obviously made an effort to turn your life around.'

My God, this was priceless. Rose Hall, the fallen woman, trying to live down her past…what would he say if he knew the truth?

Rose would have laughed if her ironic appreciation hadn't been severely dented by her response to the light seductive touch of his lips on her skin. Being this close to him short-circuited any sense of self-preservation she had left.

She pulled her hand away, but the sensitised skin of her wrist carried on tingling.

'You're offering me some sort of grudging pardon?'

Forgiveness from Mathieu Demetrios. A man who by all accounts had hardly led a blameless existence.

'That's really big of you,' she responded with a smile of dazzling insincerity. 'But for your information I haven't done anything I'm ashamed of…well, not the anything you're talking about anyway.' She stopped. 'Are you listening to me?'

The disturbing smile twitched the corners of his lips as he shook his head and confessed, 'No…I was having a Eureka moment.'

'What are you looking at me like that for?'

'I have thought of a position that you might be suited for… Yes, the more I think about it…' His narrowed eyes travelled from the tip of her glossy fair head to her toes and back again. He slowly nodded. 'Yes, you might just do.'

'Do what? What are you talking about?'

'You need a job; I need…' He paused, a smile that filled her with deep distrust spreading across his lean features. 'I have a vacancy.'

'A vacancy for what?' She had demanded a job on impulse and had not for an instant expected him to come up with the goods. She still wasn't sure he wasn't just messing with her.

'You're choosy suddenly.'

'What is this position?'

'I need a fiancée.'

In the act of brushing a strand of hair from her cheek, she froze dead. 'You need a fiancée?' she repeated flatly. He said it the same way someone else would say they needed more petrol.

'Before you get excited…' Too late, she already was if the heaving bosom was any indicator. 'The position,' he explained, dragging his reluctant gaze upwards, 'is purely temporary.'

Rose pointed to her face with a not quite steady hand. 'What you are seeing is not excitement,' she told him. 'This is fear of being in the same room as an insane person.'

The man was quite definitely off his head, but, that being a given, his mental state was apparently more stable than her own. For a split second there she had almost allowed herself to consider his offer. Not in a serious way but thinking about it in any way at all was worrying.

'If you need a fiancée I suggest you put an ad in the situations vacant column.'

Or announce it on any street corner and you'll be mobbed, she thought, watching as his lips curved into a smile that was almost as dangerous as the gleam in his incredible metallic eyes. As her eyes lingered on the sensual curve of his lips heat exploded somewhere deep in her belly and radiated outwards and downwards.

Deeply ashamed of the heavy ache low in her pelvis, she struggled to school her features into a bland mask that gave no hint—she hoped—of the physical reaction over which she had no control. The wave of colour that washed over her skin she couldn't hide; she just hoped he attributed it to anger.

'Let me explain…'

Rose didn't want explanations; she wanted the nervous excitement fluttering in her stomach and causing her mouth to grow dry to subside.

Feeling the panic rise, Rose assured herself what was happening was no big deal. It was normal. He was an incredible-looking man. It was just shallow physical attraction, nothing to get worked up about…just biology. Something over which you had no control, like a sneeze.

Think sneeze, Rose.

It wasn't easy to stand there and think sneeze when you were looking up at someone who was just possibly the most incredible-looking man on the planet.

'Save your breath,' she advised tersely. 'I'm not enjoying the joke.'

'It isn't a joke. There is a girl that my father wishes me to marry.'

Rose looked at him in exasperation. He wasn't even attempting to make this plausible.

'And you, I suppose, always do what your father wants.' She rolled her eyes, relieved that she had her hormones back in check. Mathieu being a dutiful obedient son was about as likely as him asking her to marry him for real.

'Don't,' she said, picking up her case, 'say another word. I'm leaving.'

CHAPTER EIGHT

HAD Mathieu really expected her to say yes to such a crazy idea?

'My God, I'm not that desperate!' Rose muttered, slamming the taxi door and in the process trapping the hem of her ankle-length coat in it. 'Damn,' she groaned, opening it and rescuing her coat that was now liberally coated with mud along the hem.

After a second definitive slam that made the driver wince, she slumped back in the seat and, eyes closed, exhaled a heavy sigh.

'The station, please.'

The past half an hour had all been slightly surreal.

She still wasn't totally sure if he had even been serious. If it had been his idea of a joke. People just didn't go around asking other people to pretend they were engaged. Though she was learning fast that Mathieu Demetrios was not exactly a man who felt obliged to follow the rules. In fact he seemed most comfortable making them up as he went along.

And he had a way of making the most outrageous suggestion sound almost normal. She sighed and straightened up. Pulling a compact from her bag, she flicked it open.

'If you'd stayed around a minute longer,' she told her reflection, 'you'd have ended up agreeing with him.' She rolled her eyes and laughed at her joke. Then frowned because her laughter had a slightly hollow ring to it—also the driver was looking worried.

She hadn't been tempted, not for a second.

Turning her frowning glare on the dour grey stone façade of the house as they drew away, she reached inside her bag for her mobile. The sooner a line was drawn under her Scottish misadventure, the better.

Her twin picked up straight away.

'Is this a good time?'

'Rose, of course, I was just thinking about you. How are things in bonny Scotland?'

Rose didn't waste time wrapping it up. 'Terrible. I'm coming home. As you and Nick are in New York until March, would it be all right if I stayed at your place for a couple of weeks?'

There was a pause that grew longer.

'This is where you say *I told you so* closely followed by *I can't wait to see you*.'

'Of course I can't wait to see you…'

'But?'

'But the thing is, I was going to call you, but Nick said I should leave well enough alone and…the thing is, Rose, Steven's wife is divorcing him.'

Rose's eyes opened wide.

She screwed up her face as she made an effort to visualise his face. Should a person have to make an effort to see the face of the person they had decided was the unrequited love of their life?

Even when she had formed a mental image to go with the name his eyes kept switching from blue to silver-grey and another mouth, one that was both sensual and cruel, kept superimposing itself over his.

'Are you still there, Rose?'

Rose gave her head a little shake and forced a smile even though there was nobody there to see it. 'Yes…so Steven is getting a divorce?'

Which made him available and ought to make her deliri-
ously happy.

Only she wasn't, which probably meant that Rebecca had been
right all along and whatever she had felt for Steven Latimer hadn't
been love. And *had*, she realised with dawning shock, was the key
word. Whatever it was she had felt for Steven was simply not there.

Which made her shallow and superficial—even worse than
that, he was getting divorced because of her and she could barely
remember what the poor man looked like.

'Steven is divorcing his wife?' This is all my fault.

'No, Rose, she's divorcing him.'

The hand with the phone in it fell into her lap as she sighed.
'Thank God for that.' Feeling light-headed with relief, she lifted
the phone back to her ear.

'Rose…Rose! Did you hear what I said?'

'No, sorry, I lost the signal,' she lied cheerfully.

'God, does that mean I have to tell you again?'

'Tell me what again?' Rose asked, her curiosity roused.

'Steven's wife is divorcing him because she found out that
he's been having an affair.'

'No…no, there was no affair, you were right, I—'

'Not with you, Rosie. The reptile has been having an affair
with the nanny.'

Rose's jaw dropped. 'The nanny!'

'And the thing is, Rose…' the pity in her twin's voice made
Rose half suspect what was coming next '…well, the thing is, it's
been going on for two years. I wouldn't have told you, but if you're
coming back to London you'd have been bound to have found out.'

Rose closed her eyes. 'You both warned me, didn't you? And
I didn't listen.' The memory of one of the last conversations she
had had with Nick and Rebecca before she'd left began to replay
in her head.

Rebecca and Nick had seen what he was like all along.

Eyes bleak, she lifted the phone to her ear. 'Well, it's easy to see why he found it so easy to keep his hands off me.' They were all over the nanny. She closed her eyes and allowed her head to fall forward. 'I thought his love was *pure*. Tell me, Rebecca, is there much insanity in the family? God, when I think about how he must have been laughing at me.' She scrunched up her face and swallowed the humiliation burning like bile in her throat.

'I could kill him,' Rebecca said at the other end of the line.

Releasing a strangled laugh, Rose raised her head and, phone pressed to her ear, she pushed her hair back from her face with the crook of her elbow. 'Not if I get to him first,' she said, allowing her head to sink into the backrest.

'Just don't do anything crazy. I'm catching the next plane over there. Planes do go up there, don't they? I'll ask Nick. Nick…' Rose could hear the sound of a muffled conversation. 'Nick says—'

Rose cut her off. 'Calm down, there's no need to fly over here from New York. I'm fine.'

'Liar, but if it makes you feel any better he's had the push from his job…even before the affair came out. He made a major and very costly mistake and there was no Rose there to cover it up for him.'

'I did cover up his mistakes, didn't I?' she said with a groan as she thought of all the unpaid overtime she'd put in to make sure that he looked good. 'You must think I'm a total fool.'

'Who am I to throw stones, Rose? It's not as if I have a brilliant track record when it comes to men.'

'You've got Nick.'

'I wish you had a Nick.'

'You and me both. But the Nicks of the world are pretty rare.'

'Rose says you're rare.'

'I'm unique…how is she? Tell her I'll beat the skunk up for her if she—'

Rose, who had been listening with half an ear to the conversation between husband and wife, suddenly cut in. 'I'm not.'

'Rosie,' Rebecca said, sounding worried. 'You sound really odd. You're not what?'

'I'm not coming back to London.' She didn't love Steven. The Steven she had loved had never actually existed outside her fertile imagination, but she could tell Rebecca this until she was blue in the face and it wouldn't do any good. And sympathy and understanding were the last things she needed right now. They would only remind her of what a prize idiot she had been.

What did she need? That was the question…

'So you're staying there?'

'Can't. I got the sack.' Rose barely registered her sister's shocked gasp. She was considering her options—they were rather limited. She'd sublet her flat. She wanted to avoid her sister flying back from the States, her parents' searching questions, and she was reluctant to dip into her meagre savings.

Was this the moment to throw her customary caution to the wind? Well, being cautious and doing the right thing hadn't got her very far except in the geographical sense.

'You got the sack?' Rebecca could not have sounded more incredulous, but Rose barely registered it. Her thoughts were racing.

There was a way out… Mathieu had offered it her, but it was just too crazy… She couldn't do that, *could she*? When you'd stopped waiting for Mr Right because the penny had finally dropped that he didn't exist—wasn't that the totally right time to take a leap into the unknown, and if that leap brought you into intimate contact with a man who made bits of you quiver you didn't know you had wasn't that a plus? So far avoiding temptation and being a good girl had made her a pathetic laughing stock.

She sucked in a decisive breath. 'I'm going for it.'

'You sound strange, Rose. Rose is going for it. No, Nick, I've no idea what she's going for, and will you stop interrupting? Rose, what are you—?'

'Why not?' Rose's unexpected whoop had her twin lifting the

phone with a wince from her ear. 'You're right, Becky, I'm a coward. But no more.'

'I didn't say that,' her twin protested.

'Yes, you did, and you're right. I hate being nice. Nice people just get kicked in the teeth and laughed at. You know, I didn't sleep with the wrong man because I'm too nice. Is that good or bad? I can't decide,' she mused. 'When you think about it you might as well sleep with someone you don't give a damn about because they can't hurt you and I might actually find out what I've been missing.'

'Oh, God,' Rebecca groaned down the other end of the phone. 'Are you thinking of anyone particular you don't give a damn about?' she asked warily. 'Look, Rosie, now might not be the best time to make big decisions…you're feeling hurt and—'

'I'm not hurt.'

'Of course you're not hurt.'

Rose brought her teeth together in a frustrated grimace. Her twin had obviously decided that she was being plucky and brave trying to hide her broken heart. It was deeply frustrating that nothing she could say was likely to convince Rebecca otherwise.

'There is no need to humour me. I was already completely over Steven.' Rebecca had had her 'summer to forget' before she had found Nick. Maybe she was due a winter to forget—or remember, depending on how things turned out…?

'That's great.'

'It's true—I'm not heartbroken, I'm just mad and I feel like a total idiot.'

'Look, you don't have to put on a brave face for me. I've been there. These things take time.'

'Not for me. I've met someone else.' The moment the words were out of her mouth Rose regretted introducing a face-saving lover. The chances were Rebecca wouldn't believe her anyway.

'You haven't mentioned him before…?'

'It's early days and I didn't want to tempt fate,' Rose impro-vised brightly, pretending not to hear the sceptical note in her sister's voice.

'So what's he like?'

'Like…?'

'Yes—tall, short, dark, fair? Married or single?'

'I do not make a habit of falling for married men and he's tall.' She closed her eyes and leaned back into her seat. A faint smile curved her lips as the image in her head solidified. 'Tall and very dark, with grey eyes that have a dark ring around the iris and really long dark lashes. His mouth…well, he's got a really great smile…when he does…smile, that is…'

'Wow, does he have a brother?'

The laughing query jolted Rose from her contemplative silence.

'Look, Rebecca, I have to do something and, don't worry, it's not crazy…well, it is, but good crazy. I think. I'll get back to you.' She slid the phone back in her bag and leaned forward to speak to the driver, who had been unashamedly eavesdropping. 'Could you turn around and take me back to the estate, please?'

CHAPTER NINE

'So DO you want me to wait?'

Rose took the notes from her wallet and handed them over.
'No, thanks.' She was burning her bridges—no escape route to
allow her to chicken out.

She stood, her case at her feet, and watched as the taxi vanished.
When it was gone she stayed where she was, staring after it.

'Have you any idea what you're doing, Rose?'

Good question.

She spun around. Her heart gave a lurch as she looked at
Mathieu… He represented all the reckless excitement she'd been
avoiding all her life.

And if you wanted to learn about sex he would probably be
a pretty good guide. And there would be no possibility of emotional complications because it didn't seem a big leap to assume
he wasn't into deep and meaningful relationships.

'I came back.'

'So I see. Is there a problem?'

'Not really.' Only if you count the fact I've gone insane as a
problem, she thought as his tactile voice sent an illicit shiver
down her spine… That alone should have warned her she was
making a mistake. 'I came back.'

'We covered that. I'm surprised.'

'Good surprised or bad surprised?'

'That kind of depends if you're going to take another swing at me.'

'That depends on how rude you are to me. Do you find me attractive?'

The question seemed to throw him; she suspected not a lot did.

'Or do you say the stuff you do because people expect you to?'

'Is this,' he asked, 'some sort of test? Multiple choice, perhaps?'

'It doesn't matter, you don't have to say. I was thinking…'

His winged brows lifted in the direction of his dark hairline. 'I'm not sure if I should ask…? But what were you thinking about?'

'Were you serious?' she blurted out.

'Rarely,' he admitted solemnly. 'But few people appreciate my sense of humour.'

She slung him an irritated look. 'About the job.' If you could legitimately call pretending to be engaged to a Greek million-aire a job. 'Were you serious?'

His expression sharpened. 'You'll do it?'

'Don't look smug just yet,' she warned quickly.

Mathieu watched her hair blow in the wind and struggled to control a sudden overwhelming compulsion to mesh his fingers into the silky strands…then he could draw her face up to his and… He sucked in a deep breath.

'But you're thinking about it…?' he suggested while his own thoughts stayed stubbornly fixated on the soft lush outline of her lips.

'I'm thinking about it.'

'Just thinking? Why the sudden change of heart?'

She shrugged. 'I'm assuming it pays well.'

'You expect me to believe your motives are purely mercen-ary?' He laughed, baring his white teeth in a wolfish grin.

'And what is so funny about that?'

'I meet people every day of the week who would sell their

souls for a profit margin. I can smell avarice a mile away…'
Around her the only scent he was aware of was the light floral
scent of the shampoo she used. Brow creased, he shook his head
positively. 'No, this isn't about money.'

'I'd be touched if it wasn't for the fact you were accusing me
of trying to screw money out of you twenty minutes ago.'

'I jumped to the wrong conclusion,' he admitted, drawing a
hand across his jaw.

'Jumping to the wrong conclusion is a lifestyle choice with
you. Look, do you want me to do this or not?'

Something flashed into his eyes that Rose couldn't quite put
a name to. There was a pause. 'I want,' he agreed.

Rose swallowed. 'There will be conditions,' she warned.

Amusement flickered in his eyes, but his expression was
sombre as he nodded his head and wondered who or what had
put that reckless glow in her golden eyes. 'Fine.'

'You can't say that when you don't know what they are,'
she retorted.

'When a man wants something badly enough he is generally
prepared to take the rough with the smooth.' And she was smooth,
very smooth, and he wanted her. He glanced at his watch and did
a quick mental calculation. 'I have to be in Edinburgh this after-
noon. You'll have to go on ahead to London. I'll book you on a
flight and—'

'Today? But I thought…' No, Rose, you didn't think, and that,
she reminded herself, was the point of the exercise. You're being
spontaneous. Oh, God, leaps into the unknown were a lot easier
when they weren't real.

'And on to Nixias in a couple of weeks. I'll arrange the rings
and the itinerary,' he said, taking her elbow and urging her
towards the entrance.

'What? But,' she protested as she was hustled forward, 'what
is Nixias?'

'It's where I'm going to show off my blushing bride-to-be to my family.'

'But two weeks…I thought…'

He stopped on the steps of the entrance and raised an enquiring brow. 'You thought what, *ma douce amie*?'

'What did you call me?'

'*Ma douce amie*…my sweet love,' he helpfully translated. 'Just putting in a little practice, but don't worry, you don't have to reciprocate.' Their eyes connected and a sardonic smile twisted his mobile mouth as he added, 'I'll settle for you not calling me a bastard.'

'I've never called you that,' she protested.

'Not out loud,' he agreed, casually tucking her heavy case under his arm while he dealt with the big door that swung inward with a loud creak. 'But you have very expressive eyes,' he observed, wondering what expression he would see in those eyes at the moment her climax peaked and sent ripple after ripple of pleasure cascading through her taut body.

He was not a man normally inclined to think or speak in terms of destiny or fate, but in that moment he truly believed that one day he would find out.

His molten silver eyes focused on her mouth and her eyes and hoped for the sake of his mental health that it was sooner rather than later.

'This is all so fast,' she said, stepping past him into the hallway. 'I wasn't expecting this to be so fast.'

'What can I say? A man in love doesn't let the grass grow under his feet.'

'Well, as you asked, you could try not saying that again for a start,' she grumbled, feeling the rush of blood to her cheeks.

He laughed, then said, 'Well, at least you won't have time for second thoughts.'

And he was right. The next hours flashed by in a blur: the

private flight down to London; being installed in a swish hotel suite—apparently his London flat was undergoing a total renovation—and having her dinner alone in the same suite.

That next morning the memory of the previous day's events seemed like a dream.

The dreamlike quality vanished the moment a hotel employee delivered a small red box with the compliments of Mr Demetrios.

There was an envelope with her name on it handwritten in a bold scrawl. She opened the envelope first. It was short and to the point.

'Be ready for dinner at nine-thirty. Wear this.'

He had signed his signature at the bottom. It was about as personal as a cheque, which was not a problem—she had not expected him to send love and kisses—but his Christian name would have been nice rather than the damned squiggle of his signature.

She was still frowning with discontent when she opened the box. The breath left her lungs in one shaky gasp.

On the red silk lay a ring, and not just any ring. The square-cut emerald surrounded by diamonds that stared back at her was exquisite.

Wear it, he'd said; the very thought of it scared her silly. It had to be worth a small fortune.

There was a slight tremor in her fingers as she slid it onto her left hand. It was a perfect fit. The tears that filled her eyes were, she told herself, ludicrous. It wasn't as if she were self-deluded enough to wish this were for real.

The woman who became Mathieu Demetrios's wife would have the eyes of the world on her every move. Rose wouldn't be surprised to see a candid shot of her unshaved leg change hands for tens of thousands on the open market.

While Rose was prepared to admit her take on the subject might lack balance, one thing she was sure of was that the woman who married Mathieu would have a husband other women coveted. God, she'd spend her life on a permanent diet and develop a nervous tic from keeping a watch out for younger, hungry women with designs.

It wasn't a job description that appealed to her.

She had to ring Rebecca. She would be economical with the truth, or Rebecca would be jumping on the next plane. Their parents, enjoying a second honeymoon aboard a cruise ship, she could deal with at a later date.

'It's just a marvellous opportunity,' Rose enthused.

'Marvellous. But what exactly are you going to be doing on this Greek island? For that matter, what Greek island?'

Rebecca, who had interrupted several times during her twin's rambling and deliberately vague description of her new and exciting opportunity, sounded suspicious.

'And who exactly did you say you will be working for?'

Rose hadn't, and the omission had not been accidental. She grimaced down the phone. 'Oh, you wouldn't have heard of him…the family is called Demetrios.'

'Demetrios! You're working for *the* Demetrios family?'

'It's probably a very common name in Greece.'

'Do they happen to own the island you're going to?'

'I think they might,' Rose admitted uncomfortably.

'And which Demetrios are you working for, Rose?'

'The son, I think…I really have to go, Rebecca,' she said hurriedly. 'But I'll be in touch,' she added brightly.

The dismay and shock echoed down the line as Rebecca said blankly, 'My God, Rose, you're working for Mathieu Demetrios. He used to be known as Mathieu Gauthier.'

'I think that was his name,' Rose admitted uncomfortably.

There was an audible sigh of relief. 'Then you haven't met him…if you had you really wouldn't have forgotten his name or anything else about him.' This wry aside was muttered. 'The thing is, Rose, there's something I have to tell you…'

Rose was desperate to spare her twin the embarrassment. 'Actually I've met him, but I really don't think I registered on his radar. Reading between the lines, I doubt if I'll actually see much of him once we're there.'

'Really…?' The relief in her twin's voice echoed down the line.

She hung up pleading an early night and was just putting the phone back into her bag when there was a sharp rap on the door.

'You are ready?'

She turned and saw Mathieu standing in the doorway wearing a pair of faded blue jeans, black tee shirt and worn leather jacket. The violent stab of lust that slammed through her body with the force of a sledgehammer left Rose momentarily both breathless and speechless.

The indentation between his darkly defined brows deepened as he studied her pale face. 'Are you sick?'

Rose sucked in a deep breath and thought, Oh, you have no idea how sick! But it was just physical, she told herself, determined to maintain an objectivity about the entire knee-trembling, pulse-racing thing she suffered in his presence—after all, pretending something wasn't happening implied you were scared of it.

And she wasn't; she had it under control. It wasn't as if her emotions were involved—she barely knew the man and what she did know she didn't much like.

Not like him and yet you planned to sleep with him…?

The guilty colour flew to her cheeks and her eyes fell from his.

Sanity had returned about two-thirty in the morning when she had sat bolt upright in bed, a horrified groan escaping her lips.

The only crumb of comfort she could take from this momentary madness was that Mathieu would never, *ever* know the underlying reason she had agreed to go along with his scheme. Neither he nor anyone else would ever know that she had ever got it into her head that she would throw caution to the wind and sleep with a man she didn't love, and not just any man, this man. She schooled her features into a smile and lied. 'No, I'm fine. Am I overdressed?' she asked, hating that she was asking for his approval, but it was preferable to saying she was immobilised with lust.

Mathieu's eyes, concealed from her behind the dark fringe of his lashes, slid down her body.

In his opinion she was overdressed only in that she was wearing anything at all.

He toyed briefly with and almost immediately discarded the idea of explaining to her that she was the sort of woman who looked better without clothes.

It was quite irrational to keep a guard on his tongue around a woman who he knew was more than capable of adopting the male role of sexual predator. Maybe it was because the air of wholesome sexuality she seemed unaware she exuded was tinged with vulnerability.

It was not as if he would be telling her something she did not already know. Something many men had told her before him… The thought of these faceless men who had looked with lustful longing at her lush curves brought a frown of dissatisfaction to his face.

'You look fine. I thought we'd dine somewhere casual the first night. The rest of the week, I thought…in fact, here—I made you a copy of the itinerary.'

'Itinerary?' she echoed, staring at the paper he'd handed her as she stepped out into the corridor after him.

'Unfortunately I've a full diary, the next ten days or so, but we should be able to take in a première, dinner three nights and a couple of lunches.'

'But won't people see us?' she asked as the lift door closed behind them. She took a deep breath. Oh, God, but enclosed spaces with him in were so much more, well, *enclosed*.

Mathieu looked down at her with the advantage of his superior height and shrugged. 'Being seen, Rose, is the idea. This is about photo opportunities, establishing us as a credible couple before you meet my family.'

'Oh…'

'What did you think it was about—getting to know the real me?'

The angry colour flew to her cheeks. 'Well, if you're as two-dimensional as you seem that shouldn't take long.'

'Well, if you struggle, the back page has a few pertinent facts.'

'You think of everything,' she snapped irritably. It was a good thing she had given up on the idea of seduction because Mathieu seemed to have this job laid out along very formal, businesslike lines with no room for anything more spontaneous. 'But actually you don't. I have nothing to wear at these sort of places,' she pointed out, tapping the top sheet of his so-called intinerary with her forefinger.

'The new wardrobe should be delivered in the morning.'

Her chin came up. 'New wardrobe?'

He seemed not to notice the dangerous note in her voice, though several people they passed as they stepped out of the lift did.

'If there's anything else you need don't hesitate…'

Outside in the air Rose took a deep sustaining breath and counted to ten. She'd have still been mad if it had been ten thousand. 'Listen, because I'm only saying this once, but I'm not taking clothes from you. I'm not taking anything from you.'

Mathieu threw back his head and laughed. 'Why, you sweet old-fashioned thing, you. But relax, *ma petite*, this is not a gift— it is a uniform. Don't get me wrong. I like the sexy librarian look, but not everyone has my imagination,' he drawled. 'And they will expect you as my future wife to look a certain way. When we are alone you can wear what you wish…or nothing at all…though we will have little time to be alone before we leave for Nixias.'

She could hear his laughter as she got into the waiting car. She clenched her teeth and didn't stop clenching them all evening until he said goodnight at the door of her suite.

'No, I won't come in,' he said.

'I wasn't about to ask.'

'But you did think I'd expect it?' His cynical smile deepened at her expression. 'I want my father to realise that you are not a casual pick-up, but the woman I want to be my wife.'

'You don't intend to have sex with the woman you marry?'

'After an appropriate courtship I intend to have a great deal of sex.'

Rose, her face aflame, almost threw herself through the door. 'Not with me, you're not,' she yelled, before slamming the door in his grinning face.

Rose discovered Mathieu hadn't been joking. Other than the events he had listed in his precious intinerary she barely saw him at all and as on all of those occasions they had been in the full glare of the press—she had blinked at more flash bulbs than she would have dreamt existed—it had not been exactly relaxing.

The morning of their journey to Nixias arrived and there had been only one occasion when she had seen a tiny glimpse of the real man. Or was that wishful thinking on her part?

They had been getting into a car after a meal, the paparazzi had been snapping happily, when a stray dog had appeared from nowhere. One of the photographers had tried to kick the mangy creature out of his path and that was probably the last thing he had known until Mathieu had hauled him off his feet, practised smile gone as he'd said something that had made the man's colour retreat.

'I take it you like dogs.'

Mathieu had smiled grimly and said simply, 'I dislike men who kick anything that is weaker or unable to hit back.'

If that night he had suggested coming in when they got back to her hotel suite she would have said yes, but he hadn't.

* * *

They reached the airport around ten in the morning. One brow lifted as Mathieu's silver eyes swept her face before he took hold of her left hand. 'You are not wearing your ring.'

'Not *my* ring...*the* ring. If it was my ring I'd be keeping it when this contract is over. I didn't wear it for the journey because it is obviously valuable...what if I lose it?'

'Then *obviously* you will spend the rest of your life paying me back,' he said, leading the way towards the terminal building.

Trotting on her four-inch heels to catch him up, she caught his sleeve. 'I'm serious, Mathieu,' she said. 'People who walk around with jewellery like this have bodyguards.'

'What makes you think I'm not serious?'

She met his silvered gaze, flushed and as things tightened low in her belly complained crossly, 'Don't you ever give a straight answer?'

'Relax, it's a prop.'

'You mean it's not real.' Rose didn't know whether she was disappointed or relieved.

'My father would spot a fake at twenty feet.'

'Then it is real. You father sounds scary.' Considering his son, genetically speaking this was pretty much a foregone conclusion.

'This might help,' he said.

Rose glanced with a frown at the file he had placed in her hand. 'What is this—another itinerary?'

'Some things about my father...his likes, his dislikes, things you might find useful.'

Rose, her expression incredulous, shook her head. 'Are you sure you don't want me to learn Greek on the flight over as well? Mathieu, if you wanted covert operations you took on the wrong person,' she told him bluntly. 'If I was your fiancée I wouldn't be interested in pleasing or impressing your father.'

'Just me.'

Rose pretended not to hear his sly insertion. 'It would

probably be more useful if I knew something about you other than how you like your steak and how prettily you smile for the camera. It's all so…*shallow*…'

'It or me?' he said, sounding unconcerned. 'I'm sorry if you feel neglected, but you can spend the next few days learning all my unplumbed depths.'

Rose rolled her eyes while her heart did a double flip. 'I can hardly wait,' she grunted. What had she let herself in for?

He accepted the file without comment when she distastefully handed it back to him, though he actually sounded serious when he said, 'You've got a point—it is probably best if you try as much as possible to be yourself.'

'Well, it would be kind of hard to be anyone else, wouldn't it? And what would be the point?'

He gave her a strange look. 'Most people, Rose, spend most of their life pretending to be someone they're not.'

'Well, I—' She stopped dead as she saw the private jet that was waiting for them. 'Oh, God!' she groaned. 'This is so not me. I will never carry this off. I'm just not billionaire's bride material.'

Mathieu grinned at her dismay and nodded to the man who greeted them. 'Don't knock it until you try it, *ma petite*.'

Rose slung him a disgruntled look. 'Some things, you know, don't fit without trying.'

'Oh, I think we fit perfectly.'

Not unnaturally his purred comment reduced her to red-cheeked silence. It was a silence that Mathieu seemed in no hurry to break.

By the time the private helicopter circled the island five hours later she doubted that she and Mathieu had exchanged more than a dozen words. He had been immersed in his laptop for the entire journey totally oblivious, it seemed, to her growing resentment.

It wasn't as if she expected him to hold her hand, but neither had she expected him to tune her out. Every time she had made an attempt to initiate conversation he had given a monosyllabic response. In her opinion it would have occurred to anyone with an ounce of sensitivity that she was nervous, that she required a little reassurance.

'So we're here, then.' Mathieu looked up as if finally remembering she was there.

She looked in the direction he indicated, taking in the long, low, sprawling villa built into the rock and surrounded by acres of manicured grounds.

The private jet that had brought them to Athens, the transfer by helicopter, and now the private island retreat—it was just hitting home how seriously off-the-scale rich the Demetrios family was.

Her smooth brow pleated as she caught her full lower lip between her teeth and nibbled nervously. Nobody, she thought, staring down at the island retreat—not the other guests and, more importantly, Andreos Demetrios—was going to swallow the engagement story.

Mathieu lived in a different world from the one she inhabited. She fought to maintain her calm as panic nibbled at the edges of her composure.

She slid a surreptitious sideways glance towards her travelling companion, who had abandoned his computer and was also looking through the window. She supposed the wealth thing should have been a consideration earlier. Rose supposed she hadn't really thought about it earlier because, unlike many people who needed to flaunt their wealth and position to establish their superiority, Mathieu didn't labour the fact he was staggeringly wealthy.

Not because he had any leanings towards modesty and self-deprecation. In fact, thinking of Mathieu and those worthy qualities in the same sentence made her lips twitch into a wry smile.

No, Mathieu didn't need to remind people of who he was

because he was one of those rare people who possessed a confidence that went bone-deep—a confidence that would have been there if he hadn't had a penny to his name.

Besides, far from wanting to be an object of envy or surrounding himself with fawning flunkies, he had a genuine disregard for what anyone thought about him, too arrogant to much care what anyone thought about him.

'I can see now why you don't just tell your father to mind his own business...' Honesty was the best policy in theory, but it would take an unusual man to risk losing all this.

'There's no chance of me losing all this,' Mathieu said, his voice just loud enough for her to hear above the noise. 'I own it.'

'You own what?'

'The island.'

She turned and tilted her head back to look into his face. 'You own the island...' she echoed, shock stripping her voice of all expression. Her eyes slid to the vista below and she gulped. 'All of it?' she added faintly.

He nodded and explained. 'It never belonged to Andreos, it belonged to my stepmother's family. She had originally intended that Alex and I share it, but he...' He stopped, swallowing, the action causing the muscles in his brown throat to ripple, and said, 'It came directly to me after she died.' Andreos had been furious, taking the bequest as a personal slight.

Her head was spinning. 'It didn't occur to you to mention this to me?'

He raised his brows and looked mildly surprised by the heat in her husky enquiry. 'Why should I? It isn't relevant.'

'I like that you thought it might be relevant for me to know what your father's favourite colour is but you didn't think it relevant to mention you own a whole damned island paradise.' She flung up her hands in exasperation and glared at him.

'It is only paradise now that you are here, *mon coeur*,' he drawled, clasping a hand dramatically to his chest.

Rose took an irritated swipe at him, which he evaded with a laugh. 'If you keep that up I will just laugh in your face,' she warned him, wishing with all her heart that laughter, instead of the heavy weakness that affected all her limbs, were her response to his mocking endearment.

CHAPTER TEN

'No reception committee,' Rose said, sounding relieved.

'No,' Mathieu agreed, not sounding as though he shared her relief.

She shot him a curious look. 'You're annoyed?'

Mathieu's eyes, cold as steel, flickered briefly over her face. 'You're my fiancée—not to come out to meet you is a deliberate snub.' Andreos could be as rude as he liked to him, it was water off a duck's back, but Mathieu would make sure that his father treated his future wife with the respect she deserved.

'But I'm not.'

Mathieu flashed her a strange look, then retorted, 'He doesn't know that.'

He probably will about five minutes after seeing us together, she thought, pressing a hand to her churning stomach.

'There's no need to be nervous.'

Rose tried to smile. 'And here I was thinking that I was hiding it well,' she quipped.

'Come in, it's been a long day. You'll feel better after a shower.'

It was silly, she knew, but the light pressure of his hand in the small of her back made her feel more confident.

Halfway up the path to the villa they were met by a man in uniform. He bowed slightly to Rose, then turned to Mathieu and made what sounded to Rose like a profuse apology.

Mathieu responded to him in the same language and he walked a little ahead of them the rest of the way. When they reached the entrance, a glass atrium from which several corridors radiated, Mathieu turned to her and said, 'Spyros will show you to your room.'

'You're not coming?' Hearing the sharpness of anxiety in her voice, she frowned, but she need not have worried. Mathieu appeared not to notice anything amiss.

'I need to speak to Andreos.'

She watched him stride away and tried not to feel deserted.

'Miss…?'

She turned to the uniformed man smiling encouragingly at her and followed him further into the villa.

His father was in his study. He glanced up when Mathieu walked in, then almost immediately returned his attention to the newspaper he was reading.

Mathieu walked straight across to him, grabbed the newspaper and threw it on the ground.

The older man looked at him in open-mouthed astonishment. 'What do you think you are doing?' he thundered.

'I'm laying down a few ground rules, Andreos.'

'You're laying down rules to me?" The older man gave a snort of scorn.

'Rule one…actually there is only one rule,' he revealed, flashing a cold smile that made the other man look wary for the first time. 'In future you will not slight Rose in any way; you will treat her with the respect she deserves.'

Andreos got to his feet. 'You are very sensitive all of a sudden. Who is this Rose, anyway?'

'The woman who is wearing my ring…that is all you need to know. Do we understand one another?'

'Oh, I understand you. You march in here as if you own the place.'

'I do.'

The soft intervention caused the older man's already high colour to deepen. 'If Alex had been alive none of this would be happening.'

'Alex isn't alive.'

'You were always jealous of him,' Andreos accused, stabbing a finger towards his first-born.

'If he had been someone else I might have,' Mathieu conceded. 'But he wasn't, he was Alex.' It was hard to explain but nobody could be jealous of Alex—he just didn't inspire negative emotions in people.

Or hadn't. Sometimes even after eighteen months Mathieu still expected him to breeze into a room with that grin that was impossible to resist.

'I've stepped into my brother's shoes because you asked me to, Andreos.'

The reminder earned him a dark scowl.

'But this is one area where I am not prepared to step into my brother's shoes…not even to see the Constantine fortune swell the Demetrios coffers. I will marry the woman of my choice, not someone you chose for me.'

'She's half in love with you already.'

'She thinks she is.'

And that was the problem. She'd been hurting after Alex's death and he'd been there. He'd shown her a little kindness and she had developed a crush. In the natural course of things the crush would have died a natural death. But their respective parents kept it alive by continually contriving to throw them together.

The poor kid was so vulnerable. Couldn't the old foxes see how cruel they were being to the girl? In his opinion they needed their heads banged together, but that not being an option, all he could do was not play their little game.

Hand on the door handle, Mathieu turned. 'Just don't try and manipulate me, Andreos. I don't bend.'

Outside the room Mathieu almost collided with a still figure. Hands on her shoulders, he steadied Rose before firmly pushing her away from him so that he could look into her face.

'What are you doing here?'

'I was looking for you.'

'Well, you found me. How much,' he asked, nodding towards the door behind him, 'did you hear?'

'Pretty much all of it.'

Enough to know he had loved his brother; she could hear it in his voice. She was just amazed that his father seemed deaf to his remaining son's pain. As for Mathieu's relationship with his father, that was even rockier than she had imagined. Ironically if his father had not pushed the union it was entirely possible that Mathieu would have fallen in love with the eligible Sacha, if she was beautiful, and Rose was sure she would be.

Maybe he already was in love with her?

'I didn't mean to, the door was open and…'

'You decided to listen in.'

He didn't look annoyed, which surprised her. 'Well, you weren't exactly quiet.'

'So why were you following me?'

'I asked Spyros to tell me where you were.' She nodded towards the man who was standing by the wall being selectively deaf. 'My phone was charging on the plane; you put it in your pocket. I want to ring my sister.' Want was actually the wrong word, but she did feel obliged to assure Rebecca she was all right.

'So I did,' Mathieu said, digging the phone from his pocket and handing it to her.

Rose sucked in a tiny breath when his fingertips—was the contact accidental?—brushed hers. It was easier to hide your reaction when you knew what was coming.

'You have a sister?'

She nodded, wondering what Mathieu's reaction would be if he ever discovered he had already met Rebecca.

'Just the one?'

She nodded.

'And you're close?'

'Pretty close,' she agreed, 'though she's married now, so…well, we don't see as much of one another.'

Mathieu said something to the waiting Spyros, who vanished. 'Come, you look exhausted. You should lie down before dinner.'

Rose couldn't pretend the idea did not appeal; the day was beginning to catch up on her with a vengeance. She had to make a conscious effort to put one foot in front of the other.

'This is my suite.' He pushed open a door and preceded her into a large, elegantly furnished sitting room. 'Your room is there.' He pointed towards a closed door to her left. 'And that is mine,' he added, indicating the one next to it. 'And your parents— they are alive…?'

For a moment the edit function on her vocal cords disconnected and Rose was horrified to hear herself say, 'Is Sacha beautiful?'

'Yes, she is.'

'Then why don't you want to marry her?' she wondered as she moved around the room looking at the artwork on the walls. 'Are these all genuine…?'

'I should think so,' Mathieu said, not looking at the artwork.

'You should know—they're yours.'

'Then, yes, they are genuine.' The soft wide-legged trousers she wore clung to the warm womanly curves of her hips and thighs as she moved.

'You're a beautiful woman too.'

Startled, Rose spun around, the heat rushing to her cheeks. 'Are you trying to change the subject?'

Her beauty was a subject that was never very far from his thoughts, but he judged that this might not be the best moment to mention it.

'No, I am trying to give you a compliment. Who would have thought,' he murmured, moving towards her, 'that it would be this hard?'

'Well…all right, thank you. I think,' she added cautiously. 'Why don't you want to marry her?'

Mathieu sighed and sank into an upholstered armchair. He propped his chin on steepled fingers and looked at her. 'Are we talking about Sacha again?'

'Well, if she's beautiful your children would be winners of the genetic lottery,' she mused, a frown of dissatisfaction settling on her soft features as her thoughts lingered on a mental image of golden-skinned little boys with grey eyes and jet hair. And pansy-eyed little girls with curls and sweet cupid-bow mouths.

'I think that was a compliment.'

'Like you're totally unaware that you're good-looking,' she retorted, having some sort of heat rush and not the good kind— if there was a good kind. Concentrate, Rose, she told herself, sucking in a deep breath and saying crossly, 'What are you doing?' as he grabbed her wrist and pulled her down onto the arm of the chair.

'I am looking at your neck,' he explained huskily.

'Well, don't. I don't like it.' Like wasn't the last word she would use to describe the slow-burning heat that was invading every cell in her body.

'You want to know about Sacha? I will tell you. She loved my brother. She needed someone after Alex died and I was there.'

'Your father said she loves you.'

'It is a crush, nothing more,' he said, sounding irritated. He loosed his grip on her arm and Rose got hastily to her feet.

'I think that I'll take that nap if you don't mind,' she said, backing quickly towards the door.

The interconnecting door between their rooms was ajar, Rose presumed left this way by the maid who had just brought fresh flowers into her own room.

Lips compressed, she tapped on the interconnecting door loudly. It made her feel odd to know that Mathieu could have walked in any time when she was asleep.

Not that she could imagine he would have unless he had a thing for snoring women.

'It's open.'

Rose stepped inside. 'I have a slight problem with that.'

He was standing at the window gazing out to sea.

'There is a key if you're worried for your virtue.' Mathieu, who had been standing at the open French doors, turned as he spoke.

Rose was conscious of her already tumultuous pulse giving several loud erratic thuds as it banged against her ribcage. Mathieu looked conspicuously sexy in a beautifully formal dark dinner jacket, and she barely noticed the stunning backdrop of the turquoise sea crashing onto the rocks below.

Her lashes came down in a protective sweep and she swallowed, ashamed of the silky heat between her thighs.

'And don't think I won't use it.' She could only hope he'd do the same because it would be good to have temptation removed.

And there was no point pretending that Mathieu wasn't temptation. Head tilted a little to one side, Mathieu looked her up and down. Being the subject of his silent and critical perusal made Rose's temper fizz, but she fought to control it, aware that flushed cheeks would ruin the aloof but sexy look she'd aimed for.

'Pity.'

Her head came up. 'I'm so sorry if I don't meet with your approval.' Anxious not to give him the totally false impression—she actually wanted it—she refused to ask him what was wrong with the way she looked.

'Oh, you look fine,' he said, his glance dropping once more to skim the pale blue silk shift dress she had taken a good deal of care to select.

She had also taken care with her hair and make-up and until he had turned up his nose she had been feeling confident that whatever else let her down it would not be her appearance.

Rose's temper flared to the surface as she fixed him with a hostile look. 'I look fine?' she repeated in a dangerously quiet voice.

She didn't want to look fine, she wanted to look outrageously gorgeous, although on a more realistic level she would have taken presentably pretty.

The dangerous note in her voice awoke a gleam of humour in his steely grey eyes, but his expression remained serious as he observed with a note of regret, 'It's just a pity you didn't choose something that showed…' His glance sank significantly to her breasts, which began to heave against their covering.

'Show what, exactly?'

'A little more cleavage. My father would have been too distracted to ask any awkward questions.'

'Have you never—' she choked '—heard of political correctness?'

'Heard of it, but I don't have an awful lot of time for it. Don't take it personally, Rose, I'm just being practical.'

'*Practical*,' she spluttered, practically shaking with outrage.

'I don't think there's anything incorrect in using what assets you've got, and don't tell me you never have.'

This cynical suggestion made her temper fizz. 'No, I haven't.'

She knew she shouldn't respond to his sceptical shrug

because he was obviously trying to needle her, but Rose couldn't bite her tongue.

'As for encouraging anyone called Demetrios to leer at me,' she said, 'I don't think so—just being around anyone of that name for any length of time is enough to make me want to go lie down in a quiet, darkened room.' She would have felt a lot happier if the mental image that accompanied that hot statement had her lying alone in the quiet, darkened room.

'I had no idea you felt that way…' He glanced at his watch and sighed. 'Unfortunately my father does not like tardiness. Otherwise I would be perfectly willing to oblige.'

The colour flew to her face; he had an uncanny ability to read her mind. 'I meant *alone* in a darkened room with a cold compress on my head, not you…' On top of me…inside me… What would that feel like, she wondered, to feel the weight of his hard body on top of her? His silky hardness filling and stretching her?

Glazed eyes half closed, her glance drifted to his mouth and a fractured sigh shuddered through her body. She expelled a second, deeper sigh and bit her lip. His raw masculinity and what it did to her was terrifying.

Face burning, she slammed her hand against her forehead, which even as she spoke was beginning to pound ominously.

'If you want to distract people, Mathieu, and it's legitimate to use what you've got—' and he certainly had quite a lot, she thought, tearing her eyes from the hard, supple contours of his muscle-packed torso and feeling a bit dizzy as a consequence '—why,' she suggested, sucking in a deep restorative breath 'don't you take off your shirt to go to dinner?'

She folded her arms across her chest, causing the silk across her hips to tauten, and fixed him with a tight-lipped smile.

'See how you like being treated as a sex object?'

'You would find me taking off my shirt distracting?' He was definitely finding the way the subtly shiny fabric clung to the peachy curve of her hips and thighs more than distracting. In his mind he could hear the swish of the fabric as it fell in a silken pool around her feet. The image made his body temperature rise a notch and as his imagination lingered over the soft curves the ache in his groin became more difficult to ignore.

He was asking if she would find him performing a striptease distracting…?

Rose's feeling of superiority vanished faster than her protest had the time he had kissed her. Now this was what was called shooting yourself in your own foot and then stamping on it for good measure.

She laughed nervously, her eyes sliding away as she attempted to treat his suggestion as the joke.

'One naked man is much the same as another,' she dismissed, smiling faintly.

Well, what else could she say?

She could hardly go into gratuitous detail about how she turned into a drooling, sex-starved imbecile every time she considered the hard body that filled his superbly cut clothing.

Swallowing hard, she lifted her chin and pinned a fixed smile to her face. She had heard that lust was undiscriminating, but she had not imagined how undiscriminating until she had met this man.

'So you would be bored?'

'For God's sake!' she snapped. 'That wasn't a challenge. You're an incredible-looking man with a great body,' she admitted, her attitude see-sawing between exasperation and desperation. 'But I happen not to be one of those women who go for beefcake. A six pack does nothing for me.' Well, not up to now it hadn't, anyway.

Not that Mathieu could be categorised so neatly. Beefcake was just visual candy. Nice, but instantly forgettable, and he was neither.

What he had was far more complex and dangerous than simply the combined appeal of a great body and a charismatic smile. He had an earthy sexuality that evoked an almost visceral response in her. And there was nothing even faintly contrived about it; it was as much a part of him as his fingerprints and equally unique.

A dangerous smile lurking in the back of the platinum eyes still holding her gaze, he slid the unfastened tie from around his neck. 'In that case,' he mused, 'it wouldn't bother you if I…'

Rose watched, her eyes saucer-wide in horror as he began to slip the buttons of his shirt revealing in seconds a segment of golden skin sprinkled with dark body hair. Unable to tear her eyes from the erotic spectacle, Rose ran the tip of her tongue across the outline of her full upper lip and sucked in a shaky breath as illicit excitement clutched at the quivering muscles low in her pelvis and shot down to her curling toes.

'Not in the slightest,' she agreed hoarsely. 'Although if your father doesn't like tardiness this might not be the moment to allow your exhibitionist tendencies full rein.'

'You would not find it that distracting, then?' he questioned with a show of silky smooth innocence that was in stark variance to the sensual, mocking glitter in his deep-set eyes as they moved from her parted lips and fastened onto her wide, dilated amber eyes.

Another button followed the first two and Rose, fighting for composure, felt the sweat break out on her forehead as he pulled the hem from the waistband of his trousers. 'N-not in the slightest,' she said with what she suspected was the most unconvincing show of indifference this century.

'You should never, ever play poker, *mon ange*.' His shirt hung open to the waist, revealing a large proportion of his powerful chest and a tantalising section of muscle-ridged flat stomach.

Rose was shocked and horrified by the shaft of lust that struck to the heart of her. Eyes glazed, she ran a tongue over the dry outline of her lips. The impulse to reach out and touch him, place her hands on the golden glowing skin that looked like oiled silk, was so strong she could physically taste it. She stood poised on the balls of her feet to take flight, but was unable to summon the strength to break the hypnotic hold of his smoky eyes.

Then finally she managed to turn her head sharply. Her hands clenched as she fought to calm her erratic shallow breathing and drag enough air into her lungs to stop her head spinning.

'I prefer poker to the games you play,' she husked, feeling the unexpected sting of emotional tears fill her eyes…which was crazy because she simply wasn't a crying person.

'I don't play games, Rose.' There was a note in his voice that she hadn't heard before. It made her want to search his face, but she knew that would be a bad idea. Looking at him made her mind mush…actually, her mind was permanently mush at the moment.

He covered the few feet that separated them in seconds. Framing her face between his hands, he tilted her head up to his.

Rose's knees sagged; the sexual smoulder deep in his eyes made things shift and tighten with painful intensity low down in her pelvis.

He's going to kiss me.

This alarming realisation was almost instantly followed by one that was even more alarming—I want him to!

Wanted him to so badly she could taste it—not, of course, that she was going to let him.

It would have been easy to defuse the situation—she could have laughed in his face, pulled away or told him he was taking the role play a bit too seriously. She did none of these. Rose took an option not on the list. Shaking like someone with a fever, she gave an inarticulate little moan, wove her fingers into silky raven strands of his glossy hair and dragged his face towards her.

Her fingers stayed tangled in his hair as he covered her mouth with his. She was sucking in a tremulous breath when his tongue slid into her mouth in a slow, sensuous exploration. Tugging gently at the pink fullness of her lower lip, he lifted his head slightly.

'I have been wondering how you would taste.'

The erotic, husky confidence sent a thrill of illicit excitement through her trembling body.

He freed a hand from her face to trace a lone finger along her cheek. 'I thought you might taste delicious…' He swallowed, the muscles of his throat working as he ran his tongue over the soft inner surface of her lower lip. Rose shivered and moaned softly. 'And now I know you taste even better than that…' he completed in a throaty husk.

Eyes dilated and glazed with passion, she lifted a hand to his cheek. As her fingers slid along the hard line of his cheek and jaw somehow she caught a glimpse of movement in the periphery of her vision.

The realisation that they had an audience swept through her aroused body like an icy chill; they were not alone. She would have pulled her hand away had Mathieu not held it there. Looking past her, he said casually, 'Hello, Sacha.'

'S-sorry, I didn't know…'

The girl, who was beautiful, sounded as miserable and embarrassed as she looked. If Rose hadn't been dealing with her own feelings of shame and humiliation she might have felt sorry for her.

'I just came to say that dinner…your father is waiting.'

'We'll be right there.'

The door closed and this time he made no attempt to stop her pulling away. Well, he wouldn't, would he? There was no one to see the tender scene of seduction.

And you thought he genuinely found you irresistible? Self-disgust churned in her stomach as she backed away glaring at him with loathing.

She could not, she would not, fall for Mathieu. This was just chemistry and chemistry she could deal with, she told herself. Who better? Twenty-six-year-old virgins were not renowned for their uncontrolled sexual appetites; she had reached the conclusion a long time ago that hers was underdeveloped. Any chemistry she could ignore.

'Now where were we?'

CHAPTER ELEVEN

ROSE backed away so fast she almost tripped over a low table. Hastily righting it and the porcelain figurine that she had just saved, she straightened up and hitched up the neckline of her dress a protective inch before smoothing it down.

A distracted expression filtered into her wide wary eyes as her hand remained flat on the gentle curve of her stomach. She could feel the heat of her skin through the thin fabric. Mathieu's body had felt hot when she had been crushed up against him—scorchingly hot. Hot enough to melt her.

Closing her eyes, she counted to ten—slowly. When she opened them he was staring at her.

'Was that really necessary?' she asked.

As he carried on studying her flushed face with an unsettling intensity she began to panic. What was he seeing? If he knew how and what she was feeling it would give him an unfair advantage because she as sure as hell didn't. She had never felt so confused in her life.

There was a noise outside the windows on the patio and his attention shifted briefly. Rose, who had been unconsciously holding her breath, released it on a shuddering sigh of relief.

'They are forecasting a storm tonight. It looks as if for once they are right,' he observed, walking across to close the window.

He turned as Rose was sinking into a chair. 'It felt like it at the time.' He was genuinely shocked to recognise how necessary it had felt. He was no stranger to lust, but not since his teens had he allowed it to rule him. A man could take pleasure from his appetites without becoming a slave to them.

'What?'

She looked so prim perched on the edge of the seat with her hands folded neatly in her lap. Her lips did not look prim—they looked swollen from his kisses. 'Kissing you felt necessary.' It still did.

Her eyes slid from the hunger in his; a man had never looked at her that way before.

'I'm wearing your ring.' She held out the hand in question where the square-cut emerald in its bed of diamonds caught the light. 'I think she's already got the message. That was just plain cruel,' she observed, thinking of Sacha. 'Or I suppose you'd call it being cruel to be kind…tough love…?' she ended on a sneer.

'You're shaking.'

The soft interruption cut short her heated diatribe. His voice made her shiver but not as much as his touch. As she stared at his long fingers, very dark against her pale skin, encircling her wrist, a febrile shudder worked its way along her spine, followed by a second and third as her throat dried. She closed her eyes, bit her lip and dragged herself from the fog of sexual inertia that wrapped itself around her.

'Of course I'm shaking,' she snapped, lifting her chin in an attitude of angry defiance. 'I don't appreciate being mauled for the benefit of your girlfriend.'

'You seemed to appreciate it pretty well at the time.'

Her fingers itched to slap the smugly complacent smirk off his face, they itched to do other things, but she wouldn't let herself think about those shameful impulses.

She was unable to deny the observation without looking like a total idiot—his normally sleek dark hair was still mussed from where her fingers had pushed into the rich, lush thatch. After a painful pause she played safe and ignored his comment.

'What is it about me?' she asked bitterly. 'Do I have a sign across my forehead?' she wondered, drawing a vicious imaginary line with her finger. 'Use me because I'm so stupid I'll probably just say thank you.'

The guy with the troubled sexual identity who had dumped her at the altar, Mathieu thought, a flash of contempt appearing in his narrowed eyes as he contemplated the faceless loser who was responsible for the defensive hard-faced pose, which frankly was pretty shaky.

Rose could talk the talk but he had met hard-faced, and she was not even close to it.

Whatever his faults, he had never made any promises he couldn't keep. What sort of weak idiot, he asked himself, backed away at the last minute after making someone believe you wanted to share the rest of your life with them?

Did she still love him, he wondered, this ex who had bolted? There was no trace of any emotion so tender in her face as she jabbed a finger in the direction of his chest and snarled.

'Well, newsflash, I'm not that stupid. Do you think I didn't know you were kissing me because Sacha was standing there? God, I hardly think it was necessary to go that far to get your message across.'

'You know what they say about anger, don't you, Rose? It's only fear turned inwards.'

Fear as in fear of the consequences was not a bad thing—not if it stopped you doing something really stupid. 'Very profound,' she snapped, giving him a slow handclap. 'Where did you get that one from, Mathieu, a Christmas cracker?'

'You're mad because you think I kissed you for Sacha's benefit?'

There were two tell-tale patches of colour on her cheeks as she rolled her eyes and said in a voice laced with sarcasm, 'No, I think you kissed me because I'm totally irresistible to the opposite sex.' At that moment she would have settled for being irresistible to one man, just to have the pleasure of rejecting him.

Sure, that's really likely.

Ignoring the snide voice in her head, she gave a contemptuous sniff and folded her arms tight across her chest, the action unintentionally pushing her breasts together and drawing his eyes to the modest neckline of her dress.

'I can't speak for the rest of the male sex, but you do have a seriously destructive influence on my self-control.'

Rose loosed a scornful laugh. 'What's the punchline?'

There was a pause as their eyes locked. Mathieu's voice was flat apart from a slight ironic inflection as he said, 'It isn't a joke.'

Or maybe it was, he mused. A joke on a man who had always prided himself on never being a slave to his basic instincts being so fascinated by a woman who, given the perversity of female psychology, was probably still hung up on a man who had broken her heart.

His jaw clenched as he struggled to contain the irrational explosion of anger that surged through his body at the thought of her still craving another man, he covered the space between them in one stride.

He pinned her with a molten stare and as he cupped one side of her face with his hand some of the anger seeped from him. Her skin was soft and warm...she was soft and warm. His thumb moved across the curve of her satiny cheek and with a tiny cry she pulled away.

'And you feel the same way,' he said as she swung away from him.

Rose froze, then slowly, sparks of anger flying from her eyes, she turned slowly back and planted her hands on her hips as she lifted her chin. 'Don't you dare tell me how I feel,' she snapped. 'You haven't the faintest—'

'Please,' he begged, cutting her off mid-rant. 'Don't give me that garbage about knowing Sacha was there; there could have been a twenty-person choir in full voice and you wouldn't have noticed.'

She bit her lip, knowing that no matter what she said the mortified heat was going to rush to her cheeks. Who still blushed at her age, and why wasn't there a pill to deal with this affliction?

'Because you're such a brilliant kisser, I suppose.'

'I've had no complaints so far.' His mocking grin flashed and faded. The sombre brooding expression that replaced it was even more disturbing. 'Look, I don't know why you have such a hard time accepting what is obvious, and there is an obvious solution. Sleep with me.'

Rose didn't say a word. She couldn't. The embarrassed flush that had coloured her face fled, leaving her deathly pale as her shocked gaze flew to his. If you took away the tension around his jawline there was absolutely nothing in his expression to suggest he had just proposed anything more momentous than picking up her dry-cleaning.

She would have treated it as a joke and laughed if her vocal cords and facial muscles had not frozen solid.

'Think about it.' Again his manner bordered on the offhand, but then deciding to have sex with someone was probably nothing he got worked up about…neither presumably would he lose any sleep if she said no…which obviously she was going to…

Responding to the pressure of the hand in the small of her back, Rose began to walk towards the door.

CHAPTER TWELVE

'SORRY we're late.'

There were seven people sitting around the table. Following the lead of the heavy-set grey-haired figure, presumably Andreos Demetrios, at the head of the table the men rose courteously as Rose approached.

It would seem he had taken Mathieu's demands to heart.

Rose carried on smiling—it could be that the pasted smile might have to be surgically removed at a later date—as Mathieu made the introductions.

It was always hard walking into a room of strangers. Walking into a room of strangers when you were pretending to be someone you weren't raised the stress stakes a hundredfold. But she was not, Rose realised, nearly as nervous about being the focus of six pairs of critical eyes as she was at the thought of being alone with Mathieu once dinner was over.

What was she going to say?

Andreos gave her a hard assessing glance. She smiled faintly back. If she hadn't been so distracted by the scene in the bedroom still playing in her head she might have managed a token display of the deference that Mathieu's powerful father obviously considered his due.

Now of course she could think of a hundred responses ranging from amused to cuttingly sarcastic that would have left Mathieu in no doubt that she was not interested.

Instead what had she done? Nothing. Nothing was only slightly less incriminating than the truth, which was his suggestion had excited and scared her. She hadn't said anything because she had been afraid that if she opened her mouth she might hear herself say something along the lines of, Yes, please.

The knowledge appalled her.

'Well?'

Rose, about to take her seat, stopped and glanced towards her host. She saw the flash of annoyance in his face. Damn.

'My father asked if we had a good journey.'

'It was an experience. I'm not used to travelling in such luxurious style.' She turned her head as she lowered herself into the chair that Mathieu held out for her. Their eyes brushed before he straightened up. She found his expression hard to read. He seemed tense. Did he think she'd gone out of her way to annoy the older man?

Besides the two cousins who were like paler, less bulkier versions of Andreos Demetrios, there was the man himself, an aunt, a lawyer who had been introduced as a family friend, the lovely Sacha and her mother, a thin woman who drank water and pushed her food around her plate.

The mother looked at Rose with a marked lack of the warmth and animation that was in her face when she addressed Mathieu, who sat opposite Rose.

Sacha's expression when she looked at Mathieu was equally transparent. Rose found it difficult to believe that Mathieu could be as indifferent to her shy adoration as he appeared. The younger girl looked gorgeous in a dress that showed off her smooth pale gold shoulders. The moment her glance lighted on the glowing young brunette, Rose felt like an ancient and overweight frump.

'Not hungry, Rose?' Mathieu asked in a voice intended for her ears only as he leaned towards her.

Rose's own hushed voice had a shaky quality due in part to the shock of having her foot nudged, which might have been accidental if her shoe, an elegant high-heeled court, had not been slipped off. There was nothing accidental about the fingers that curled around her ankle.

'I…' Rose gave a yelp as the fingers slid higher, and drew her foot back, blushing deeply.

'I bit my tongue.' She sent a look of seething reproach in Mathieu's direction while nodding fervently to the maid with the wine bottle who had materialised at her elbow.

She was beginning to suspect she'd need whatever prop was available to get her through this meal.

By the time the fish course was served Rose's initial discomfort had been replaced by a tipsy recklessness.

She was wondering if anyone would actually notice if she got up and left, when Andreos's deep voice cut across the quiet and slightly stilted chatter of the dinner table. 'So my son tells me that you met in Monaco.'

Rose lifted her eyes from her plate.

As she put her fork down on her plate Rose could hear the beat of her pulse in her throbbing temples. Her eyes moved past and beyond Andreos to Mathieu who was sitting directly opposite her.

She wondered for the umpteenth time since they had arrived how she had allowed him to talk her into this.

'Oh, I love Monaco,' she heard Sacha bubble happily. 'It's just about my most favourite place in the world.'

'I've never been there,' Rose said in a clear voice that carried around the table.

Mathieu didn't express panic or even moderate concern that she wasn't playing the game. Rather his lips quivered and she saw the amused glitter in his eyes before he bent his head, calmly reapplying himself to the food on his plate.

Rose, her eyes narrowed, looked at his dark head with dislike.

A man who had gone to the trouble of inventing a fiancée and kissing her senseless in front of a witness to prove a point ought, under the circumstances, to look less relaxed when it looked as if his elaborate charade was about to be blown.

Andreos, his manner interrogative, turned his attention to his son. 'She says—'

Mathieu's dark head came up. The warning reflected in his eyes was mirrored in his deep voice. 'She is called Rose, and she is sitting beside you.' His eyes swivelled in Rose's direction. 'I hope, *ma petite*, that you will forgive my father. He does not intend to give offence, but he manages it anyway.' His attention swivelled back to his father, who looked ready to explode at the thinly veiled censure.

Andreos opened his mouth to deliver a robust denunciation but Rose got in before him.

'Genes being what they are,' she retorted, reminding herself that Mathieu was only playing a role when he rode to her defence.

Not that she needed anyone riding to her rescue—she could look after herself. A notable exception to this rule of self-sufficiency being when she was about to drown in the middle of an icy loch. There were moments that she forgot that she owed him her life.

'It would have come as an enormous shock to me if *your* father had turned out to have manners that could be called faultless.'

The jibe drew one of Mathieu's lopsided and wildly attractive grins. His father was a few beats behind in interpreting her comment. When he did his jaw literally dropped. With no experience of guests who told him he was rude, he struggled to come up with an appropriate response, though she could see that his natural instincts leant towards throttling.

'Young woman—'

'Rose,' Mathieu inserted.

'Rose, you seem to be a very outspoken young woman. That no doubt is what attracted my son to you, but I do not appreciate—'

Mathieu's languid drawl sliced across his father's rebuke. 'No, I'm shallow—her ability to speak her mind was way down the list.' His grin broadened as his eyes slid suggestively down her body.

Rose, her face flaming, dropped her fork. It hit the floor with a clatter. 'I hardly think your father is interested.'

'Such innocence. Of course he is interested, Rose. I would be most surprised if there isn't a firm of private investigators working round the clock in search of salacious details. By tomorrow he will know your shoe size and favourite colour. I could have saved you the trouble, Andreos—there is nothing that you could tell me about Rose that would shock me.'

She thought he was joking until she saw the Greek entrepreneur's expression. The colour seeped from her face at the idea of strangers building a dossier on her; it made her feel physically sick.

'So you didn't meet in Monaco. I suppose you're not engaged to be married either,' Andreos said, not denying his son's charge.

'I wouldn't marry him if he was the last man alive,' Rose announced to the room at large.

There was a startled silence, broken when Mathieu put down his fork, threw back his head and laughed.

His reaction made everyone present treat her comments as a joke.

Rose glared at him with seething frustration.

'I'd be grateful in future if you did not bring your lovers' tiffs to the dinner table.'

'You're right.'

Andreos looked visibly startled by his son's agreement.

'Forgive us, it is not an appropriate place to air our differences. I can promise you,' Mathieu continued, his eyes holding Rose's, 'that it won't happen again.'

'Don't you dare apologise for me,' she breathed wrathfully. 'And,' she added, her gaze swivelling in the direction of the older

Demetrios, 'this is *not* a lovers' tiff,' she gritted from between clenched teeth. 'We are not even…' She stopped. She couldn't think the word in the same context as Mathieu, let alone say it out loud.

'Not even what?'

'Lovers,' Mathieu inserted.

The suggestion of unspoken intimacies in the warm velvet undertones of Mathieu's deep voice brought a rush of colour to Rose's face. The resulting laughter dissipated the tension around the table. People began to eat once more.

Mathieu didn't. He laid down his fork and looked directly at Rose. Her heart began to hammer as she read the message glittering in his platinum eyes—a combination of challenge and something more elusive.

With a last glare of fulminating loathing at his amused dark face she stared fixedly at her plate until the fragrant lamb was a misty blur.

She could not have said what else she ate during the interminable meal and when it was over the ordeal went on. The women retired to the salon.

Rose found the segregation slightly Victorian and the conversation stilted and awkward.

It could not have been much more than five minutes before Mathieu left the other men who were gathered on the terrace and came to join her indoors, but it felt like longer to Rose.

As he crossed the room looking like the archetypal dark brooding hero of fiction her heart started to throw itself against her ribcage. The sudden hush that fell amongst the chattering women and almost audible buzz of interest made it clear that hers wasn't the only heart to misbehave.

And was it any wonder? Even if you left the drooling sex appeal he oozed out of the equation, aesthetically speaking he was very easy on the eye—even the way he moved was riveting.

He touched her shoulder as he reached her side and left his

hand there, a proprietorial gesture that she had no doubt was for the benefit of the other women. 'It's been a long day.'

She nodded and wondered if there was any way she could make him move his hand without making it too obvious his touch was so disruptive to her nervous system that, given the opportunity, she would have crawled out of her skin to escape the nerve-tingling sensation.

His attention lingered on her face. 'You look tired,' he observed, sounding very much the attentive lover, and then the forceful lover as he announced casually, 'We will have an early night.'

Teeth gritted and trying very hard not to think about what an early night with Mathieu might entail if the circumstances were different, Rose responded to the pressure of the hand that was under her elbow and got to her feet.

An image slipped past the barrier. She wasn't sure if the groan was in her mind or if it had actually come out of her mouth. Then she saw the way everyone was looking at her—question answered.

The edges of Mathieu's deep velvet voice were roughened with concern as he searched her face and asked, 'Are you all right?'

She shrugged off his hand. 'Did it occur to you that I might not want an early night? I'm quite capable of deciding when I want to go to bed and,' she added grimly, 'who with.' She didn't add that normally the choice was between a good book and the cat from across the way that always came calling when she left her bedroom window open.

'The truth? No, it didn't occur to me,' he admitted. 'But don't worry—I take rejection well.'

'Like you'd know.'

To Rose's relief—she was still biting her tongue—Mathieu didn't react to her as good as telling him that he was too gorgeous for any woman to resist. She bit her tongue to stop herself explaining that she was an exception to the rule. She was, after all, meant to be engaged to him and, besides, it might just smack of the lady protesting too much.

'Rose,' he explained for the benefit of the women who were straining to catch each syllable of this lightning-fast exchange, 'is trying to reform me.'

'Reform?' Sacha, her dark curls bouncing attractively as she turned her head quickly looking in bewilderment from one to the other, echoed.

Rose could see the girl's dilemma. As far as she was concerned it was a case of why reform what was already perfect, and from the way her eyes followed Mathieu it was clear that she thought he could not be improved upon.

'It is her ambition to drag me into the twenty-first century,' he explained, 'and turn me into a modern man.'

Sacha flushed and lowered her eyes when Mathieu directed his ironic grin in her direction. Her mother, however, was not similarly tongue-tied.

'A modern man,' Helena Constantine echoed, her artfully pencilled brows lifting as she gave a contemptuous smile. 'Despite what they may say all women prefer strong men, not a puppy dog.' From the direction of her admiring stare it was not difficult to see whom she was talking about.

Rose rolled her eyes. 'For goodness' sake, it's not like he needs encouragement.'

The older woman's carmine lips tightened in response to Rose's flippancy. She glanced at Mathieu and seemed disappointed when, far from looking outraged, he was openly amused.

'A man should lead, a woman should follow,' she said firmly.

'Not this woman,' Rose promised, quite enjoying the novelty of finding herself cast in the role of staunch feminist. 'I'm not the following kind.'

'Mama says that the trick is making a man think the idea was his in the first place,' Sacha confided, glancing towards her mother for support, her smile wobbling slightly when she saw her parent's expression. 'She says that a clever woman can make a man do…' Her voice dried up totally in the face of an icy glare from the older woman.

It was Mathieu who came to her rescue.

'There you have it, a clever woman…that leaves you out, *mon ange*.'

There was nothing faintly angelic about the expression on Rose's face as she asked, 'Are you calling me stupid?'

'I have far too much respect for my well-being to call you anything of the sort. How fortunate it is I prefer feisty women to the clever variety,' he said, looking straight at her with an expression that in her mind was inappropriate outside the privacy of a bedroom.

'And as for turning you into a modern man,' Rose said, forcing herself not to break eye contact even though her stomach was churning with a volatile mixture of excitement and heart-racing fear, 'I'm a realist.'

And as a realist she knew that he was acting a part. He really didn't want to rip off her clothes, send the crockery crashing to the floor and make love to her on the table. Oh, yeah, Rose, hold that thought. It's really going to help you stay calm and in control.

'As a realist I don't attempt the impossible.'

'How about…?'

Rose closed her eyes. His manner suggested he had just had an epiphany, while the gleam in his eyes told her he was about to say something that would make her want to curl up and die from sheer mortification.

Unfortunately her reading of that gleam turned out to be spot on.

'If in the interests of harmony once the bedroom door is closed I will let you take a turn being in charge…'

A choking sound emerged from Rose's throat. Of course she was delusional to have thought even for a second that she could get the better of Mathieu in a war of words; he would always win in the end—he had no scruples.

In the sybaritic image playing in her head he had no clothes either. The only thing covering his gleaming golden skin was a fine sheen of sweat and her thighs where she sat astride him. She blinked and sucked in a shaky sigh as she tried to block the treacherous thoughts that made her skin crackle with heat.

'You like the idea?'

Rose liked the idea of a deep dark hole opening up at her feet for her to step into. She had never felt so embarrassed in her entire life. She flashed Mathieu a look of appeal, which he responded to with a warm and loving smile. Lowering her gaze, she gave a theatrical yawn before announcing she was actually quite tired.

She didn't meet anyone in the eye as she bid her fellow guests a hurried goodnight and headed for the nearest door.

CHAPTER THIRTEEN

SHE had gone a couple of hundred yards before Mathieu caught up with her. 'Well, I think that went well,' he observed with some satisfaction. 'Don't you?'

She stopped dead and spun around to face him. Had he been in the same room as she had?

'Went well! No, I don't damn well think it went well. I think it was a total nightmare and so were you.'

His long lashes swept down to partially conceal his eyes, but not before she had caught the wicked amusement dancing in the silvered depths. 'Did I say something to upset you?'

The innocent act made her grind her teeth. Did he get a kick out of baiting everyone or was it just her he liked to see squirm? 'Now what makes you think that? I just love having people think I'm into, into…bondage or something.'

There was startled silence before his warm laughter boomed out. 'I admit I am having trouble seeing you as a dominatrix.'

His taunting grin widened when she lifted her hands to her burning cheeks and choked, 'Shut. Up.'

'Relax,' he advised. 'I imagine they are simply thinking we have a healthy sex life.'

Relax. Was he serious? It was bad enough that her own imagination was running riot without the thought of other people speculating about what they got up to in the bedroom.

'You think that makes me feel better?' she asked. 'You may like to discuss your sexual preferences with all and sundry, but I prefer my sex life, even my imaginary sex life, to stay private.'

'It can hardly be private from your lover. Who is your lover, Rose?'

The twin bright spots on the apples of her cheeks deepened to carnation pink. 'I can't imagine a situation where that information would be any of your business.'

His sardonic smile widened and she got a flash of even white teeth. 'You can't…?'

'And it just so happens I don't have a lover,' she blurted. 'I've never had a—' She stopped dead and developed a sudden interest in the patina on the marble floor.

'Never what? Had a lover?'

She listened to him laugh softly at the idea and gritted her teeth. 'Now you know my little secret.'

His eyes drifted to her full lips. 'And now I'd like an answer to my question…' It was not the only thing he wanted… He had never in his life wanted a woman this much. He thrust his hands in his pockets to hide the fact he was literally shaking with need.

'What question?' She stopped as their eyes meshed. Mathieu raised one brow and gave a savage smile as he watched the colour climb to her cheeks.

'Oh, *that* question.' She dredged a laugh from somewhere. 'Don't worry, I didn't take you seriously.'

'Yes, you did, and I was serious, deadly serious.'

It was hard to maintain her flippancy in the face of his steady and disturbing silver stare but she did—just. 'Look, Mathieu, you're not paying me that much.'

His upper lip curled. 'Name your price. I might be willing to meet it.'

Something inside her snapped. Her response was pure reflex.

There was no conscious thought between lifting her hand and it connecting with a resounding crack with the side of his face.

'Oh, God, I'm so sorry…' Tears sprang to her eyes as she watched him rub a hand over the area on his cheek that was already discolouring. 'No, I'm not sorry, you deserved that. You've progressed from implying I'm some sort of tart to treating me as one.'

Mathieu's hand fell away. 'Yes, I did deserve it. That was an unforgivable thing to say and I'm sorry.'

The anger faded from her face. 'You are?

He nodded. 'It's no excuse, but I'm extremely frustrated.' He placed a hand on the wall beside her head and leaned in, his smoky eyes drifting slowly across her face.

Her chest felt so tight she could hardly breathe as two opposing instincts battled inside her. The sane area of her brain was telling her to back away; another was telling her to lean into him.

Rose couldn't back away because there was no place to go— her back was literally against a wall. The only thing preventing her from taking the second course was a fragile thread of control, but as the heat in her stomach spread and the hunger spiralled that control was stretching to breaking-point.

'Mathieu,' she groaned, turning her head and kissing the finger he trailed across the cushiony softness of her lips. 'You're…this is…' She swallowed, her eyes drifting to his mouth. She was willing him to kiss her when the distinctive sound of voices raised in laughter drifted down the corridor. The sound seemed to mock her.

What was she doing? With a horrified squeak she ducked under his confining arm and began to walk away at speed, praying as she did so that her knees would not buckle.

His chest rising and falling in tune with his rapid, shallow respirations, Mathieu watched her walk away. In some women he might imagine that the sexy sashaying sway of the hips was contrived, but not Rose. There was no calculating flirtation or fluttering eyelashes with her.

It seemed incredible to him, but she was genuinely oblivious to the fact she represented to the opposite sex a sexual ideal, the sort of woman that they dreamt about waking up beside in the morning.

No wonder he lost all sense of perspective around her—the woman was a mass of contradictions.

She had jumped naked into his bed and now she blushed like an inexperienced adolescent if the conversation turned to anything remotely intimate.

She showed him a cold face and claimed not to be interested in him sexually. Yet he knew she was lying. He knew she felt the crackle of sexual tension between them as strongly as he did. He had seen her eyes dilate until they were black pools, felt her body tremble at the accidental brush of their fingers and felt the heat under her cool exterior.

Had her idiot ex been too self-absorbed to teach her to enjoy her own body and celebrate her ripe sexuality? Humiliated by him, she had lost her confidence and tried to recapture it by getting drunk and having casual sex with a total stranger—him. Had his own rejection that night been the act that had made her retreat?

He raised his voice and called after her. 'You didn't read the small print, Rose. No time off, not even for good behaviour, and, let's face it, you were not good back there.'

Breathing hard, Rose swung back, her eyes dilated as she found him standing almost at her shoulder. 'I never said I'd lie for you and there is no small print, nor any print. You're just making up the rules as you go along.' She ached to wipe the taunting smile off his face, and it wasn't a recognition that violence solved nothing that stopped her, but a suspicion that if she touched him for any reason it might be hard to stop.

'You know what I think?'

'I'm shaking with anticipation.'

She was shaking too, Rose realised, registering with a scared frown this new development. Anger, she told herself. She was shaking with anger.

'I think things are going exactly to your plan. You don't want your father to approve of your bride.'

'Interesting theory. Just why would I want my father to disapprove of my future wife?'

'Because you take a sadistic pleasure out of doing the opposite of what he wants you to.' Before she actually said it Rose didn't have the faintest idea what she was going to say, but even before she saw the flicker of shock move at the back of his eyes she knew that she had intuitively hit the nail on the head.

'My father…'

'Oh, he's just as bad as you are, I can see that. I'm really not concerned with who did what to who.'

To hear his complicated and painful relationship with his father reduced to the level of a school-yard squabble reduced Mathieu to a stunned silence.

'I just want out of it.' She bit her trembling lip, cleared her throat and added in a flat voice, 'You chose me because you knew that I'd never fit in.'

Now why should that hurt so much?

Shaking his head, Mathieu reached out his hand. Rose pulled back, her eyes wide and wary. With a shrug and a twisted smile he let his hand fall away. His eyes were flint-hard as he said dismissively, 'I didn't choose you. This was an arrangement of mutual convenience, though I have to admit there has not been a lot of convenience involved so far. The irony is that you were the perfect choice.' His considering glaze slid over her. 'If I had turned up with one of the usual suspects…he would have smelt a rat immediately.'

'Usual suspects?'

'Well-groomed, articulate…'

'Everything I am not, presumably.'

'Oh, you scrub up pretty well.'

'You know, there being nothing in writing works both ways. If I choose to walk there's nothing you can do to stop me.'

'You underestimate my resourcefulness…'

She stuck out her chin. 'But not your total lack of scruples and ruthlessness.'

Mathieu's brows drew together in a dark disapproving line above his hawklike nose. 'That's what most people say about my father.'

Ironically it was the familial likeness that he appeared offended by, not the insult… Not that this mattered to Rose— her objective had been to annoy him.

'Most people haven't been forced to spend as much time in your company as I have recently.' She could think of more than a few who would pay for the privilege.

He pretended not to hear her muttered interruption and angled a curious look at her face. 'My father…you're not scared of him, are you?'

'Scared?' An image of the broad-shouldered Greek financier flashed through her mind. 'Why should I be?' Now his son, that was another matter. She turned her head sharply and gave a little shiver as her eyes brushed his profile.

'He's rich and powerful.'

'He has nothing I want or need—why should I be afraid of him? You, on the other hand…'

'You think I'm afraid of my father?'

She had expected the suggestion to produce an offended denial, but the only reaction she got was an amused quiver of his lips.

'I suppose you think fear is a sign of weakness.'

'No, I think fear is healthy.'

'Oh, will you stop sounding so impossibly well balanced? You made your living tied down in a metal box hurtling around in circles while people paid money for tickets to watch while they waited for you to crash. Someone who chooses to make their living that way—' she tapped the side of her head '—has a few screws loose.'

It was the families she felt sorry for—the ones who loved those men who risked their lives…and for what? The thrill, the money, the fame…or was it cheating death that hooked them? Either way it was the wives and mothers waiting at the sidelines that had her sympathy.

'I…' Mathieu closed his mouth with an almost audible snap, shock quickly followed by caution filtering into his expression as he realised what he had been about to do.

Why should he feel the need to justify his life choices, redeem himself in her eyes? Why, when he never asked for anyone's approval, should Rose's good opinion matter so much to him? A man who normally did not duck issues, but met them head-on, he found himself pushing this particular issue to the back of his mind.

'It was something I was good at.'

She lifted her eyes in mock amazement. 'You mean there are some things you're not good at? I thought you were brilliant at everything. Except,' she added with a wry twist of her lips, 'being pleasant to your father.'

'*Me*. You think it's my fault?' The resentment he told himself he had put aside along with other childish things surfaced and his jaw clenched.

'Well, it takes two, doesn't it? And you can't deny you don't go out of your way to be nice. There's an atmosphere you could cut with a knife when you're together.'

'He thinks the wrong son died.'

Mathieu, the most alive person she had ever met, dead. She shook her head in violent mute rejection of the idea and saw the floor moving up towards her.

She gave a sigh of relief when the world steadied, but didn't loose her grip on the ornately inlaid console table she had grabbed on to to steady herself.

Of course he regretted saying it the moment it left his lips. He sounded like someone looking for the sympathy vote and nothing could be farther from the truth.

He regretted it even more when he saw Rose's amber eyes fill with compassion.

She was just the sort of woman who would go for the damaged type, he thought irritably. It wasn't by accident that the women he ended up having relationships with did not want to heal or mother him.

Mathieu was scowling but, more significantly, he was avoiding her eyes. He wouldn't look at her—was he afraid of what she would see?

She felt like yelling, Your father hurt you, big deal, join the rest of the human race. She also felt like wrapping her arms around him and pulling him close, but she knew he was a man who would not appreciate the gesture.

No, that would mean admitting he wasn't totally invulnerable.

'I'm sure he doesn't think that,' Rose said, wondering why it was that some men found it so hard to talk about their feelings. Half the family rifts in the world would be healed if men actually did more than grunt and look noble. 'It's not like he actually said that…' She paused, her eyes sweeping his dark face. 'He did!' Her soothing expression melted into one of angry indignation.

How could any man, no matter how much he was hurting, say something like that to his own son? She'd like to give the selfish old man a piece of her mind.

'Alex was the exact opposite of me.' He made it sound as though this was a reason, an excuse even.

'Why does the memory of your brother have to push you apart? That's the one thing you and your father have in common,' she pointed out, shaking her head in exasperation. 'You both loved him.' You'd think that would draw people together, not push them farther apart.

'Look, I didn't bring you here to bring about a reconciliation between me and Andreos. I'm not paying you to be an agony aunt.' He saw her flinch and hardened his heart against the hurt in her liquid-gold eyes.

Rose stiffened. 'Don't worry, I won't forget my place again.'

'Your place is not in my head.' He clasped a hand to his head and gave a frustrated groan. 'Oh, for God's sake, don't look at me like that.'

'Where is my place, Mathieu? Just so that I know.'

His burning eyes swept her face. 'In my bed, damn you,' he said, turning on his heel and striding off.

CHAPTER FOURTEEN

ROSE knew Mathieu was in the room even before her nostrils flared in response to the scent of his body. His invisible presence was like an electric prickle under her skin.

'You've been crying.' The visible damage, her red-rimmed eyes and the tear marks on her cheeks made something inside him twist.

'I always cry when I get mad,' she said, keeping her eyes trained on the waves whispering on the moonlit shore. Behind her breastbone her heart was beating like a captive bird and as the last lingering effects of the wine at dinner had worn off she couldn't even blame that for her response.

'Did you cry because you thought I wouldn't be back?'

His voice warm like honey came from just behind her. Paralysed by the insidious weakness that was spreading through her body, she managed a negligent shrug and suggested coldly, 'You forgot something?' She turned her head and he nodded.

She wanted to look away but she couldn't stop staring. His glossy dark hair was sexily mussed as though he had just run his fingers through it. His jacket was gone, and his tie hung loose around his neck. But it was his eyes that made her stomach dissolve; they were burning like molten silver.

She cleared her throat, but the words wouldn't come. Her restless gaze moved over the shadow on his jaw following the line of his strong neck to the base of his throat, and lower then to the section of satiny golden skin revealed where the top buttons of his shirt had parted.

She sucked in a deep breath and stuck out her chin as she gave a shrug…a yawn would have been overkill, especially as she had a horrible suspicion he knew exactly what havoc he was wreaking on her nervous system.

The extra gust of wind that blew in from the sea ruffled his hair and made her shiver. The distraction enabled her to pull free of the sensual thrall that had held her immobile.

She turned her back on him and closed her eyes. 'Then get what you want and leave.' *Before I touch you…* In her fevered imagination she already was; her hands were on his ribcage and sliding lower to his flat, muscle-ridged stomach. She put a stop to her treacherous thoughts…

'That was my intention.'

She felt the warmth of his breath brush the side of her neck. A shiver of excitement chased a path down her spine as her heavy eyelids closed.

'What are you waiting for?'

Her eyelids lifted abruptly when a moment later he took her by the shoulders and spun her around to face him. The lines of his face were taut with anger and frustration.

'I'm waiting for you to stop pretending this isn't happening.' He looked down at her; the devouring hunger in his spectacular eyes sent a violent surge of bone-melting lust through Rose's receptive body.

'Nothing's happening except I'm catching a cold standing in this draught.'

He lifted a hand and made a stroking motion that traced the outline of her head but did not make contact, although her nerve endings reacted as though he had.

His voice normally had nothing more than the faintest trace

of an accent, but when he spoke it was now thickly accented. 'Your hair looks silver in this light.'

Rose swallowed and shook her head. Things were moving too fast. At this rate the point of no return would have passed without her explaining that this wasn't what she wanted.

It was, of course, but that was irrelevant. As intellectual exercises went, the one where she had felt empowered and daring enough to plan being seduced by a man she had no emotional connection with—a man like Mathieu—now seemed totally ludicrous.

For starters there was nothing intellectual about the things the scent of his warm body did to her. The danger in him aroused and excited her. Primitive, raw instincts, she was discovering, were not something you could intellectualise, and as for no emotional connection… As much as she wanted to believe he had just woken dormant sexual instincts within her, Rose knew what she was feeling was far more complicated than simple lust.

A sensible woman like her didn't waste feelings on a man who had no use for them.

And she was sensible…wasn't she? A month ago she would have had no problem replying in the positive, but now she knew, and it was a shocking realisation, that if she let herself she could fall in love with him… The question was could she stop it happening, and did she actually want to?

But those were questions for later; her mind could not deal with them now.

'And your skin looks like moonlight, so soft, so smooth.'

The throaty rasp shuddered through her and though she struggled she couldn't tear her gaze free from the burning silver of his deep-set eyes as they devoured her. A tremor rippled through her body as his fingertips grazed the side of her cheek. She closed her eyes and shook her head, desperately trying to cling to some semblance of self-control and sanity.

'I don't know why you're trying to fight it. We have no control. It is coded into our DNA.'

'Do many women fall for that "it's just chemistry" line, Mathieu?'

The lines of his chiselled face tautened with anger. 'I'm saying that what we are feeling is as basic as the colour of our eyes. You may not like it but you have to live with it.' His glittered like liquid silver as his restless glance roamed over the soft contours of her upturned features.

'Convenient fatalism, but I don't have to live with you and I definitely don't have to have sex with you,' she retorted.

There was a glow in his eyes that was sinfully suggestive as he bent close to whisper in her ear, 'Great sex.'

His sensuous purr had a catastrophic effect on her sensitive stomach muscles. She plucked at the neckline of her dress as her skin prickled with heat. Her heart thudding with nervous excitement, she swallowed and shook her head.

He drew back a sound that was close to a growl vibrating in his chest as he ripped the loose tie from his neck and threw it on the floor. 'Are you trying to tell me that you don't want to share a bed with me?' Actually the way he was feeling—the closest words in his extensive vocabulary that came anywhere close to describing that condition were *totally out of control*—meant the bed was by no means a prerequisite. Just about anywhere would do.

The urge to feel his skin in contact with her skin was overwhelming. If he wasn't able to satisfy the primitive instinct to sink into her softness and warmth and feel her tight around him it was possible he would lose what little sanity he had left.

'Well?'

The words of denial shrivelled on Rose's lips the moment she met the smouldering challenge in his. She swallowed and squared her shoulders.

'Just because you want something doesn't make it a good idea.'

'And you want me.' He closed his eyes as a shudder of relief vibrated through his lean frame.

She doubted he could have sounded any more smug or complacent if he'd tried, but it was hard to feel the proper level of indignation over this when he couldn't have looked more sexy or desirable either.

And on that front, to give the devil his due, he never tried, he just…

'If you don't, just lock the door.' Producing a key from somewhere, he held it out to her.

Rose caught her full lower lip between her teeth as she stared at it.

After a moment the key went the same way as the tie.

'You can hardly stand up, you're literally shaking and I haven't even touched you.' He swallowed, his voice dropping a husky octave as he added, 'Have you any idea what it does to me to know that? To know that you're weak with lust for me?'

'I am.' Rose stared into his eyes, seeing her own reflection there along with the combustible mixture of the emotions that gripped him.

Her heart was beating so frantically that she could hardly breathe as she lifted a hand to touch the spot in his lean cheek where a nerve jumped. He turned his head and caught her hand, pulling it to his lips, drawing one finger and then the next into his mouth.

A fractured gusty sigh escaped her lips and her knees disintegrated. She would have fallen in a heap at his feet if he hadn't caught her at the last moment, wrapping an arm around her waist and drawing her upright.

Her heavy lids closed and she gave a dreamy sigh, savouring the tensile strength in his lean body, conscious of the febrile shudders that intermittently shimmied through the length of his body.

'Are you all right?'

'I'm amazing,' she said, tucking her head into the angle

between his chin and shoulder. She had never imagined that weak and helpless could feel so liberating.

She felt the soundless growl of laughter vibrate in his chest. 'Well, amazing Rose, I think we should take this discussion into the bedroom.' His urgency intensified, as did the ache in his groin as he anticipated the touch of her bare skin against his. His urgency deepened as he imagined her body closing tight around him. 'Right now,' he added, bringing his other arm around her waist and hauling her higher and closer against him.

Feeling the pressure of his erection against the softness of her belly, she gave a startled, '*Oh*,' and her eyes flew open. As she gasped for breath her eyes connected with the heat in his and she melted some more. '*You're* incredible.'

Rose had never in her life felt the primal drive, the need to be possessed by a man. But she had been fantasising about being possessed by Mathieu Demetrios from the first moment she had set eyes on him. Maybe he was right, maybe it was about something programmed into her genes, but frankly she didn't care.

It didn't matter, she realised with a sense of relief—she had moved beyond the guilt, the tortuous heart-searching and trying to make sense of it.

Even if this was the worst decision of her life she was going to make it happen… Even if she spent the rest of her life regretting it, she wanted Mathieu so much it was more important than breathing and just as essential for her continued survival.

For the first time ever she understood the real meaning of all-consuming passion. She had met the love of her life and she might not be destined to spend the rest of her life with him, but she was going to savour every moment that she did have.

'How can you be surprised? You must know how much I want you.'

'Tell me,' she whispered in a husky voice he had to strain to hear.

He expelled a long deep breath and said, 'I'll show you.'

She let out a small shriek as he cupped her bottom and lifted her upwards. As he swung her around and began to stride towards the bedroom door she wrapped her legs around his waist and, pressing her breasts against his chest, linked her arms around his neck.

She fitted her mouth to his and kissed him hungrily, opening her mouth in response to his probing tongue, and groaned into his mouth as the kiss deepened. When she came up for air her fingers still curled into the hair on the nape of his neck.

They were both breathing hard as they stared into each other's eyes.

'You're staring,' he said thickly.

She nodded. 'At your mouth. I think,' she mused, 'that it is one of my most favourite things in the world.' It was strange not to be censoring her words, strange in a good way.

'Your mouth is in my top ten,' he admitted, 'and, while kissing it is even higher, you do realise that if you carry on doing that we're never going to make it to the bedroom.'

'Beds are good, but the floor is fine.' Did I really just say that?

'True, but the thing is I've been imagining you naked with your hair spread out over silk sheets since the moment I met you.'

He'd been imagining her, imagining her being some red-hot lover… Rose's insecurities came crowding in. She really ought to tell him up front there was every possibility she would be rubbish…enthusiastic but rubbish.

'What's wrong?'

For once she wasn't dismayed by his ability to read her thoughts. 'I don't want to make a mess of this.'

She leaned close so that her nose almost grazed his, her nostrils quivering as she inhaled the musky scent of his arousal overlaid by the light citrus tones of the obviously expensive cologne he favoured.

He was so totally delicious, everything about him fascinated and excited her.

'Not possible.'

'You say that now, but—'

'Shut up.'

He was kissing her so she didn't have very much option and, anyway, about two seconds into the kiss she forgot what she wanted to say. A second after that she forgot her own name.

Still kissing her, he carried her across the room to the bed where he laid her down. Then not taking his eyes off her, he began to remove his clothes, the task made more difficult by the fact his hands were shaking so much.

He had fought his way out of his shirt and kicked off his trousers when she sat up and stretched her arms out to him. Not able to resist the invitation in her glorious golden eyes another moment, he knelt beside her on the bed.

Rose struggled to catch her breath, her throat ached…he was so beautiful he made her ache all over. Just looking at him burnt her up from the inside out.

Mathieu took the hands extended to him and turned them over. 'I want your hands on me,' he rasped, his voice as dark as the hot feelings inside her.

A fractured sigh snagged in Rose's throat as he laid her hands palm down on the bare skin of his tautly muscled belly. Breathing shallowly, she raised herself up on her knees and slid her hands up over his hair-roughened chest. Circling his tight male nipples with a finger, she leant forward, repeating the action with her tongue.

His skin tasted salty; he tasted the way he smelt.

'Sweet mother of God,' he groaned, sinking his fingers into her hair and dragging her face up to his. His hands framed her face. 'Look at me,' he said thickly. '*Dieu*, but I want you, Rose.'

Her eyes slid to his mouth. Just looking at the sensual curve made things tighten and shift low inside her. 'What's stopping you?' she asked, thinking, I love you…oh, God, I love you.

They kissed fiercely with a bruising desperation, fighting to deepen the contact. Mathieu's hands fell to her hips and he jerked her hard to him, sealing their bodies at hip level, letting her fully appreciate the urgency of his throbbing arousal.

Rose could feel the tremors running through his greyhound-lean frame. 'I didn't know anything, anyone could feel this way.' Her head fell back as his lips moved down her neck, his tongue flicking across the pulse throbbing at the base of her throat.

She pulled back and looked at him, and he smiled a slow smile that felt like a fist tightening very deep in her belly… Her skin burned in an agony of anticipation as he slid down the zip of her dress and, still holding her eyes, peeled it gently off her shoulders.

When the fabric pooled around her waist revealing her full pink-tipped breasts he sucked in a ragged breath. 'You are beautiful, *mon coeur*,' he rasped, weighing one perfect breast in his hand before bending his head and running his tongue across first one engorged peak and then the other.

Desire like a flame licked through her body as her back arched. She found the sight of his dark head against her pale skin incredibly, mind-blowingly erotic.

He was speaking in French, the hot, impassioned words spilling from his lips as he pushed her back against the pillows and spread her hair like a golden curtain around her flushed face. He then curved her arms above her head, his eyes darkening as he watched her breasts quiver, the peaks hardening as they lifted.

'Is this the way I looked in your fantasy?' she whispered, forcing the husky words past the aching emotional thickness in her throat.

He smiled, a fierce smile that thrilled her to the core. 'You are my fantasy, *ma petite*.' One hand gently splayed across her abdomen, he pulled her dress down over her hips until she lay there in a pair of lacy pants. He ran a finger along the pale smooth flesh of her inner thigh and she trembled, gasping his name as his fingers continued to stroke and tease, releasing a flood of heat that washed over her heated skin tingeing it with a faint rosy blush.

'Don't stop,' she pleaded when his fingers lifted from her skin.

She felt rather than heard the deep laughter vibrate in his chest, but when he bent over her and locked his eyes onto hers there was no laughter in his face. There was strain evident in the sharp-drawn lines that drew the skin tight over his incredible bones and a hungry, almost febrile glitter in his deep-set eyes.

'There is no possibility of that happening,' he promised huskily. Then, turning away briefly, he divested himself of his boxers. She watched him through half-closed eyes, one arm thrown above her head in an attitude of wanton abandon.

When he turned back her eyes dropped. A stab of sexual heat shot through her body all the way to her curling toes.

'Oh, my,' she breathed shakily.

She wanted him so much her skin crackled with it, her blood hummed with it. She couldn't put the depth of her longing into words, but she tried, and she wasn't even embarrassed by the inarticulate babble that came from her lips as he moved over her, parting her thighs and trailing a finger along the silky soft skin of her inner thigh, drawing sharp gasps and moans of pleasure from her throat before moving higher and deeper into her moistness.

A keening moan stayed locked in her throat as she moved against his hand.

Nothing, she thought, could be better than this.

She was wrong.

Her body arched as he thrust into her and a wild cry of startled delight left her lips.

Above her Mathieu froze and, between rasping gasps, growled, 'Look at me.'

Rose's mind, every part of her, was so totally concentrated on the incredible sensation of being filled and stretched by him, the heat of him, the smooth thickness of him, that there was a time lag before she responded.

Eyes glazed, the amber colour of the iris reduced to a thin

strip, the pupils were so dilated, she blinked up at him, momentarily blinded by the luminous glow in his.

He stared down at her, his golden skin coated by a glistening coat of sweat, the sinews in his clenched jaw and neck standing out as he struggled to hold himself in check.

'You're…you're…'

I'm dying, she thought as her head began to thrash from side to side on the pillow. Unable to bear the pressure building up inside her—there was nowhere for it to go—she pleaded, 'Please, Mathieu, please…'

Then as she felt him pull back she tried to lift her head and cried out in alarm. 'No…no, I need…'

She grabbed for his shoulders, her fingers sliding over his sweat-slick skin, then her nails sinking in to hold him.

She breathed a fervent sigh of relief as he slid back into her, not deeply enough to satisfy the hunger inside her, but enough to send shafts of shimmering sensation coursing through her body.

He repeated the sequence again and again, pulling back with agonising slowness, then sinking in each time a little deeper until she could feel the rhythm in her head, in her blood, in her bones—she couldn't separate herself from it.

When it got too much to bear she prized her eyes open. 'Mathieu, I can't, this is…I need—oh, God, I can't bear it,' she moaned.

He looked into her passion-glazed eyes and a groan was dragged from deep inside him. 'Neither, *mon coeur*, can I,' he groaned, thrusting deep into her, giving her all of himself.

She responded with a wild cry, wrapping her legs tight around his waist and pushing up to deepen the glorious penetration and the intense nerve-stretching pleasure. Her breath grew shallow and fast as she felt the pressure build, then as the light exploded behind her eyelids she went limp and let the shattering climax claim her.

Mathieu felt her pulse tightly around his length and with a groan let go, and with one final thrust a feral moan was ripped from his throat as, gasping for breath, he collapsed on top of her.

CHAPTER FIFTEEN

AS THEY lay there intimately entwined, in a tangle of sweat-slick limbs, Rose smiled and ran her hand down the damp curve of Mathieu's back.

'I am the first man you have been with.' Rolling off, Mathieu lay on his back, one hand curved over his head. The knowledge lay like a stone behind his breastbone. He stared at the ceiling as he added hoarsely, 'How is this possible?' The question seemed addressed more to himself than to her.

Rose, still floating on a cloud of languid contentment, felt the first stirrings of unease filter into her bliss. She opened her eyes to look at him through the damp screen of her lashes.

Back-lit by the shaft of light from the half-open curtain, his tautly muscled torso gleamed like oiled silk and Rose was overwhelmed afresh by the spectacular beauty of his powerful body. Emotion locked the muscles of her throat tight.

'Speak to me, Rose…'

She lifted a hand to her cheek and felt the salty wetness of her tears. She had not been conscious of crying. 'So you're my first—does it actually matter?'

Mathieu looked at her in astonishment. 'Does it matter?' he echoed in outrage. 'You were an innocent.' He swallowed, causing the muscles in his brown throat to ripple visibly as he fought to contain his feelings, unable to believe she could not understand how this altered everything.

'A damn virgin…*Dieu*…' He lifted a hand to his head and fell backwards onto the mattress.

'You were the one who said I'd never had a lover.' Her attempt to draw a smile failed miserably. When his head turned on the pillow towards her she could almost physically see the waves of tension rolling off him.

'I was being ironic and you knew it,' he bit back before he closed his eyes once more.

He had done everything right up to this point. So why did he have to spoil everything now? 'I really think you're in danger of blowing this way out of proportion.'

'Every word you say,' he told her through gritted teeth, 'is making this worse.'

'Fine, I won't say anything.' She felt his rejection like a physical pain in her tight chest. Face white, she rolled onto her stomach, dragging the sheet up to cover her nakedness, nakedness she had just minutes earlier taken voluptuous pleasure in. Now it was all ruined, her hot skin began to cool and she shivered.

She had found their love-making so incredible, more mind-blowingly perfect than she could have imagined possible, that it had not occurred to her until he had begun to speak that he had found the experience less satisfactory. Which, when she thought about it, was not so surprising as she had not known what she was doing, but it had felt pretty good at the time.

He dragged a hand across his eyes. '*Dieu*, what have I done?' he groaned.

'You want me to explain? I thought I was the innocent?'

He turned his head, the anger in his eyes smouldering. He looked as angry as she had ever seen him. 'I hardly think that this is the moment to be flippant.'

The dry laugh locked in her emotionally constricted throat.

'Believe me, I do not feel flippant. If you expect me to apologise for being pretty amateur, forget it.'

'You have some explaining to do,' he told her heavily.

'No,' she said, pulling herself upright. The sheet still gathered around her, she swung her legs over the side of the bed, presenting her stiff, straight back to him.

'The woman I found in my bed in Monaco was not a virgin.' His thoughts flicked back to the aborted seduction scene, his dark brows drawing into a frowning straight line as he shook his head positively. 'Definitely not!'

'How would you know? I thought you threw her out of your bed.'

Rose let out a squeal of protest when with no warning a brown arm snaked around her middle. Clutching tight to the sheet, she fell back across his lap. Lying there, looking up into his lean face, she felt the hunger so recently sated stir.

'A man knows these things.'

'You didn't know these things about me,' she reminded him.

A nerve clenched along his jaw. 'I'm waiting, Rose.'

'I don't owe you anything, least of all an explanation,' she husked, her chest rising in tune to the rapid gusty breaths that escaped her parted lips.

Her angry contention made him stare. 'You were a virgin,' he said rawly.

'Will you stop saying that? It's not like I planned to be a virgin at twenty-six. I just wanted to be sure…' She stopped, aware of the implication of her words, and retrieved the situation by adding with a laugh, 'And then I suppose I just gave up waiting.'

'And I happened along. You know how to make a man feel special, *mon coeur*.'

'Stop calling me that,' she snapped angrily. 'You've got a cheek acting as if I've tried to pass myself off as something I'm not.' It was painfully obvious that he would have preferred the sexy siren she had turned out *not* to be. He would have preferred Rebecca, which made him no different from every other man. 'I never said I was that woman—in fact I've never stopped saying that I wasn't her.'

'But you knew that I thought…'

The condemnation in his manner struck Rose as wildly irrational and it frustrated the hell out of her that he couldn't recognise the fact. 'And I thought enthusiasm would make up for lack of experience. It looks like we were both wrong,' she countered. 'For goodness' sake, it's bad enough you're making me feel like a cheap one-night stand, but do you have to rub salt in the wound by making me feel like a cheap one-night stand who is useless at sex? If I'd known that you only sleep with women with a diploma in fornication I would have—'

'This is not about you being inexperienced in bed.' He looked at her with total incredulity. The women he had relationships with were as selfish as him; with them he knew where he stood. It infuriated him that she could act as though what she had given him was inconsequential.

Rose struggled upright and sat there on the edge of the bed with her back to him. 'Not much,' she grumbled, trying to imply with her small laugh that she found his reaction faintly amusing. The last thing she wanted was him even starting to suspect that she was totally devastated.

'Oh, for goodness' sake, can we just drop the subject and agree it—' she gestured without looking at the tumbled bed-clothes '—was a mistake.' And what a mistake! Her soft lips twisted into a wry bitter smile as she added, 'I'm not the woman you wanted. I'm not the woman from your hotel room.'

'I did not want her, desire her…you…' His glance slid down the curve of her rigid spine. His brow furrowed as he tried to tackle the conundrum presented to him. 'You are identical… Even your voices…' One he desired, the other left him cold. He stopped dead, a spark of startled comprehension appearing in his eyes. 'There are two of you...*twins*...?'

Rose dodged his now-angry gaze and began to pleat the sheet between her fingers.

Mathieu muttered something in French under his breath, pulling her around towards him with one hand, and pushing back the locks of hair that concealed her face with the other. His hand stayed there framing her face. 'Look at me,' he commanded, tilting her chin up to him. 'That woman in Monaco, she was your sister, your twin, wasn't she, Rose?'

Rose nodded. There seemed little point in denying it.

He expelled his breath on one long, sibilant sigh.

'And she is the one who was jilted at the altar.' His eyes swept her face and Rose gave a tiny nod. 'The one who went off the rails,' he added, his voice and manner getting angrier with each additional suggestion.

'She's married now to an absolutely lovely man.'

'And do you know this from personal experience too?'

Rose shook her head in bewilderment. 'I don't understand.'

'Well, you seem to share most things.'

A wave of angry colour washed over her skin as the implication sank in. 'You have a really nasty mind—you know that, don't you?'

His hands fell away. His head sank forward onto his chest as the layers of implication hit him. 'I know nothing about you,' he said, lifting his head and looking at her blankly. 'You are not the person I thought you were.'

'The person you thought I was?' she repeated, the bubble of anger inside her bursting. This was meant to be a memory, a perfect moment for her to recall in years to come, and he had spoilt it with his interrogation. 'How can you be so hypocritical?' she asked him.

'You deceived me and it is *my* fault?'

'I haven't deceived anyone,' she yelled. 'I told you until I was hoarse that we'd never met before. And I don't see the problem. Do you normally want to know a girl's history before you have sex? You're a total hypocrite. Five minutes ago you weren't even vaguely interested in the person I am beyond my bra size.' From the direction of his gaze the same thing was still true.

With an angry snort of disgust she brought her hands up to cover her heaving breasts. 'Oh, I'm not criticising you for being shallow, I knew that you didn't care about me, but to turn around and act as though I have somehow cheated you, well…' She shook her head energetically enough to send strands of caramel hair whipping around her face.

'You are calling me shallow?'

On another occasion Rose might have been amused by the expression of stark incredulity written on his lean face.

'I can see why you're so upset. You must have thought I was ideal for your purposes. A woman traumatised by a painful romantic experience.'

Teeth clenched, he ground out, 'You are suggesting that my *modus operandi* involves taking advantage of vulnerable women?'

Rose was not deceived by his soft tone. She doubted she had ever seen anyone as angry as he was right now. On another occasion she might have been cautious about her response, but she felt strangely disconnected from what was happening as she stared at the nerve clenching and unclenching in his hollow cheek.

'I'm saying a woman who was just dipping her toe back in the water after getting burnt.' Even as she said it she recognised that you could drive a cart and horses through the analogy. Any woman who thought Mathieu was a little light relief, a safe place to get back into the dating game, would be seriously unbalanced.

'And you were—just dipping your toe in the water?'

He waited for her response, glaring at her as though this was all some part of her fiendish master plan.

'I suppose I got tired of waiting for Mr Perfect. You see, I thought I was in love, but he was married and I thought honourable, but he was just using me. I found out the day you offered me this opportunity…' She gave a shaky laugh as her gaze slid across the tumbled, still-warm bedclothes. 'I really don't think this is what the graduate career service had in mind when they talked about opportunity.

'I had this mad idea that it would be a good idea to find out about sex with someone I didn't care about.'

'So you approached this like a scientific experiment?'

'For God's sake,' she exclaimed. 'It lasted for about two minutes before I wised up. I admit I was curious what everyone was going on about. What I'm trying to say is I'm not really in a position to judge your motives.' He obviously did not feel similarly restrained.

'You are not the person I thought you were.'

'Can you hear yourself? I'm not the person you thought I was. As if you'd know.' She released a hard little laugh. 'You didn't know the person I was; you didn't know anything about me. What could you know about the person I am?' she asked him. 'The person I *really* am,' she added, pressing her hand to her heaving bosom.

'You didn't sleep with me, Mathieu, because you liked who I am or even who you thought I was, because I am the person you have been looking for all your life. You slept with me because I'm here and available and you thought I'd be low maintenance. Well you can relax.'

Her advice did not seem to have any immediate soothing effect. He looked about ready to implode.

'I'm out of here as soon as I can thumb a lift.' The trouble about an island was a grand sweeping exit was hard to achieve.

Dragging the sheet from the bed, envying him his total obliviousness to his nakedness, she stood up and walked towards her bathroom.

Inside she lasted until she had locked the door, where she slid down the wall to the cold marble floor. Where in a foetal huddle she cried until there were no tears left.

She didn't know if she would have opened the door if he had asked, but her resolve was never tested because Mathieu didn't knock and when she crept out in the early hours the suite was empty.

'You might as well unpack,' Mathieu said, entering the room and glancing down at the suitcase she had left by the door. 'Nobody is leaving this island today.' Did it make him insane that he would lie just to have her the other side of a wall, soft and lovely and hating him?

'Then why is that helicopter out there?'

His eyes slid from hers. 'You may think I have delusions of grandeur, but even I can't control the weather.'

'Or me,' she told him, registering for the first time the wetness that had his clothes clinging wetly to his body and his hair slicked back and drenched. 'Helicopters don't stop flying because of a bit of rain.' She picked up her case and willed him to say something to stop her. But of course he didn't because basically he couldn't wait to see the back of her.

'The ring is on the dressing table. Oh, and don't be surprised if your father looks smug when you see him.'

'Oh?' he said, studying her expression with a frown.

'We had a breakfast meeting. And I've made him really happy.'

'He has clearly not done the same for you.' The clenched teeth and flashing eyes were the clue.

'He offered me money to leave you. You don't look surprised that your father tried to buy me off,' she accused, studying his expression. 'Does he do this often?'

'It was not something I had anticipated, but I should have. If he is happy, I'm assuming that you said yes?'

'Not immediately. I negotiated. After all, you are a very rich prize for a dedicated gold-digger like me.' Her teeth ached as she held the fixed white smile in place.

'Would it be indelicate to ask how much I'm worth?'

'I wouldn't give a brass farthing for you.'

'No, you did make clear to me last night that your only interest in me was…' he swallowed, struggling to keep a lid on his anger '…scientific.'

'I never was very good at chemistry.' But he was—her eyes dropped—very good. 'Actually I can't remember how much we settled on. I was angry,' she admitted with admirable understatement. 'Here,' she said, taking it out of her pocket with a shaking hand and shoving it at Mathieu.

Mathieu smoothed the scrunched paper. His brows lifted as he read the figure above his father's distinctive scrawl. 'You are a good negotiator,' he said, handing it back to her.

'You think I want that?' she said, looking from the cheque to him. 'You're as bad as he is.'

'You might as well keep it. The money means nothing to him and you have earned it.'

Rose felt strangely removed from what was happening as her hand began to move in an arc. It wasn't until it met his cheek with a resounding smack that sent his head sideways that she registered what she had done.

'This time I'm not sorry,' she said. 'And if you're ever in town be sure not to get in touch, because I promise you there is more where that came from.'

She swept out, the image of his grey furious eyes imprinted on her retina.

The helicopter was over the grey stormy Aegean before the first sobs were torn from her chest and she doubled over in pain.

CHAPTER SIXTEEN

'THIS is your first scan?'

Rose, feeling a light-headed mixture of trepidation and excitement, nodded as she lowered herself on the high bed. Maybe some of the former showed because the woman in the white coat explained in a soothing manner, 'We've had a cancellation, the appointment following yours. I could wait for Dad to arrive if you like?'

Rose swallowed as weak tears rushed to her eyes. With a tight little smile she struggled to regain her composure. 'No, he won't be coming. He's—'

'Right here.'

Rose's head turned; her expression went totally blank. Shock froze her mental faculties as she stared in disbelief at the tall figure framed in the doorway.

Had she finally lost it totally? Was she hallucinating?

Her eyes locked on platinum-silver and the colour rushed back to her face the same moment her brain began to function. This was no hallucination; this was something much more dangerous—the real thing. A hundred questions swirling in her head, she chose the cautious option and asked suspiciously, 'What are you doing here, Mathieu?'

Mathieu's brows lifted. 'Where else would a man be when the mother of his child is having her first scan?'

'America?'

Escorting long-stemmed American beauties who did not present him with the tedious burden of their virginity she tacked on silently.

She had read the story of his proposed trip in the financial pages. For a supposedly serious journalist, the woman who had written it had been almost gushing in her praise of the man she said would bear watching.

But then who was she to talk about lack of objectivity? she thought. She was the idiotic woman who had cut out the article and kept it.

She sucked in a deep sustaining breath, telling herself she could do this. Actually she could do little else but stare at him as though she was afraid if she blinked he might vanish.

'America? No, as you see, no…I am here.'

At that moment the shrill sound of a bleeper broke the expectant silence in the room.

The radiologist reached into the pocket of her white coat and shared her apologetic smile equally between the two prospective parents. 'I'm sorry. I'll have to take this…I won't be long.'

Rose, who had levered herself up into a sitting position, watched the woman go and barely restrained the impulse to beg her to stay.

She cleared her throat. 'I really don't think you being here is such a good idea, Mathieu. Not really…appropriate.' She gave a weak smile and touched her stomach. 'I'm pregnant, you know. It was quite a surprise.'

He gave a dry laugh and dragged a not quite steady hand through his dark hair. 'For me too, Rose. You do know that you can't do this alone…?'

His woman giving birth alone, having his baby alone… His chest swelled as he fought to contain his emotions. This was just not going to happen, not while there was breath in his body. If she didn't love him he would make her…if necessary he would change.

'God, no, I'm pretty clueless, but the staff here are absolutely terrific and I'll see the same midwife all the way through to the birth, build up a relationship…'

Listening to her, Mathieu bit back a frustrated groan. Spitting hostility, he reflected, would have been easier to deal with than being treated with this stilted politeness. 'I think it's our relationship we should be concentrating on. Don't you, Rose?'

She still wasn't totally sure that he wasn't a figment of her imagination, but when he bent forward there was nothing imaginary about the lips that brushed her forehead before claiming her mouth, or the warm, clean scent of his male body.

The light kiss left her breathing hard and aching.

'We don't have a relationship, Mathieu.'

He stood, his hands resting either side of her. 'But we have a baby.' He cupped her chin in his hand and tilted her face up to him.

'How do you know the baby is even yours?' It was a ridiculous thing to say, but she felt pushed into a corner.

'Are you saying it is not?'

'No, I'm not saying that,' she admitted reluctantly.

'Good call. It is always good to keep deceit within shouting distance of the truth.' Something he had not been doing when he had told himself that he could function perfectly well without one Rose Hall.

'Is it so impossible that I might have had sex with a man other than you?'

'Frankly, yes.'

'Well, you didn't find me so repulsive once,' she retorted, stung.

Amusement flared and died in his eyes to be replaced by a simmering heat. His eyes darkened with desire as they swept over her face. 'You are the most desirable woman I have ever seen in my life, Rose.'

Her head spinning dizzily, Rose's eyes fell from the warmth in his. 'If you had found me repulsive I suppose we wouldn't be here now,' she conceded shakily. 'Not,' she added hastily, 'that I'm blaming you.'

His mouth curled into a grimace of self-recrimination. 'Who else would you blame?' he wanted to know.

'Well, you hardly had to beat me into submission with a stick, did you? And we…you were careful.'

'But accidents happen,' he added on quietly. 'I'm not angry about this, Rose, if that's what you think.'

'No, you're resigned,' she accused in a quivering voice. Resigned enough to ask her to marry him? And if he did would she have the strength to say no?

'The reason, Rose, I know you haven't slept with another man, leaving aside the lack-of-opportunity factor, is firstly because it is not in your nature to have casual sex—it is not a mechanical act for you, you make *love*—and secondly you do not want another man…just me.'

This display of male arrogance drew a dry laugh from her aching throat. 'Do you know how that sounds?'

'It sounds true.'

Rose glared up at him. 'I suppose you think you've spoilt me for any other man…that I'll spend my life comparing all other men to you…' Well, if he hadn't thought it before he was in no doubt now—way to go, Rose.

'You won't have to. I'll be right here for you.' He ran a finger down her cheek and Rose, her skin tingling and her heart aching, jerked away.

'Of course you will.'

And they both knew why, she thought dully. She had always known this was going to happen when Mathieu found out about the baby.

Which made her prepared…or *should* have, because he was reacting exactly as she had anticipated. He was doing everything in his power to prevent his child growing up without a father as he had.

And he was obviously willing to do whatever it took to bring that about.

He was even prepared to pretend to love her. A flicker of raw anguish crossed her face at the thought.

The awful part was she was tempted—tempted to take what he was saying at face value and not question it. It would be easy to rationalise, there were a lot of pluses, the baby would be secure and loved…Mathieu would be a great father. She would wear his ring, share his bed, and wait for the day he came home and admitted he had fallen in love for real.

She firmed her jaw and took a deep sustaining breath. Her baby deserved better. A lot better than a mother so pathetically desperate for the love of a man who didn't return her feelings that she was willing to live a lie.

'I can't wait to see you grow even more lusciously lovely carrying our child.' He ran his hands down her bare arms and she shivered. 'We will do this thing together, *ma belle*.'

He knows what you want to hear, she reminded herself, and he's saying it. She attempted a laugh. It wasn't her most convincing effort, but it did bring a flash of baffled frustration to his face.

'How did you even know there was a baby?' Her brow furrowed. This ought to have been her first question.

'You mean it was a secret?'

His brows lifted in mock incredulity, but behind the cynical mocking smile that curved his lips Rose saw anger lurking.

'And here was I thinking I was the only one not in the loop.' Mathieu was unable to keep the bitterness from his voice.

'I haven't told anyone. I've barely got used to the idea myself.' Rose was annoyed to hear the note of apology in her voice.

'You've known long enough, according to your sister, to decide that you don't want me in your life full stop. I think,' he mused, 'that was roughly what she said, give or take the odd assorted insult concerning my birth.'

Rose's jaw dropped. '*Rebecca* came to see you…but she and Nick are living in New York.'

'I've been in New York for the past couple of months, Rose.'

Rose buried her hands in her face and groaned. 'Oh, my God, I'll kill her. She promised me.'

'She did mention something along those lines, but she felt, and I have to say that under the circumstances she was right, that the situation warranted a little deceit. When exactly did you intend to let me in on your little secret…or did you not plan to?' His jaw clenched, he struggled to contain his anger. He wasn't the injured party here, he reminded himself grimly.

'Look, I would have told you first, but Rebecca is my twin and…she just knew.' The twin thing was a bit hard to explain to someone who didn't have firsthand experience. 'It must have been a bit of a shock.'

'I didn't get the news directly from your sister. She was still crossing town when Andreos rang to tell me you were pregnant.'

The moment his words registered, the colour fled her face. 'Your father?' Rose, her eyes wide with horror, lifted a hand to her mouth.

He nodded. 'Rebecca had apparently turned up at his hotel looking for a Demetrios to castigate and got the wrong one… She arrived at the right hotel just as I was leaving to catch the flight here. It's possible that I might have upset her.'

Rose responded to this admission with a grim smile. 'Good.' Why did her twin, who was barely five minutes older than her, think she had the right to interfere in her life as and when she deemed necessary? She slanted a curious look at him and wondered, 'How did you upset her?'

'I had a plane to catch and time was running along; your sister is quite fond of the sound of her own voice. So there came a point when I had to bring the conversation to a close.'

'You're not saying you threw her out…*again*?' Despite everything, Rose's lips twitched at the mental image.

'I showed her the door.' And it had barely closed when Andreos had banged on it. It had felt to him at the time that fate was conspiring to make him miss his flight, though thanks to the skill of a cab driver who gave a new meaning to fearless he had caught it. 'I was polite…well, *fairly* polite,' he amended. 'It was not easy.'

'Why?'

'Your sister kept telling me that I slept with you because I thought you were her…'

'You did think I was her.'

A spasm of exasperation flickered across his lean face as he framed her face with his big hands and left her little choice but to look at him. 'Well, that is one thing that you have in common: you are both stupid.' And the most stupid thing he had done in his life was letting Rose walk out of it. Well, that wasn't going to happen again.

Before Rose could object to this scathing observation he added, 'I told your sister that if I had wanted to sleep with her I would have when she offered.'

A minute before Rose had been thinking some pretty unkind things about her sister, but it didn't stop the reflex to fly to Rebecca's defence kicking in at the first hint of criticism from someone else.

'Don't run away with the idea that Rebecca was behaving normally when she—' She broke off, shifting uncomfortably in her chair under his sardonic scrutiny.

He arched a dark brow. 'When she what?'

The flush on Rose's cheeks deepened as she glared at him resentfully.

'Propositioned is, I think, the word you are searching for,' he inserted helpfully. 'The polite one, anyway. But don't worry— Rebecca was anxious to put the record straight on the subject. Apparently she couldn't have been in her right mind at the time because I am not her type.'

Rose stopped short of calling her twin a liar, but she couldn't prevent the sceptical snort escaping her throat before her teeth clenched. In her opinion Mathieu was every woman's type.

'I assured her that this was mutual and the reason I didn't take what she offered was because I *was* not and *am* not attracted to her.' His lips twitched slightly as he confided, 'She was not inclined to believe me.'

Neither was Rose. She could not imagine why he would not be attracted to Rebecca. Despite his protests, she knew that Mathieu had been enchanted by Rebecca. All men were.

'That,' he mused half to himself, 'is something you do not share…'

He was running the tip of his forefinger very gently across the curve of her upper lip and it was actually quite hard to respond at all, but she managed a husky, 'What is?' before her eyes closed, and a deep sigh shuddered through her body.

But pretending that she wasn't wildly attracted in a fatal moth-to-a-flame sort of way had never been a serious option. And Mathieu knew exactly what effect he had on her. But had he realised yet that she was in love with him?

She gave a fatalistic sigh. If he hadn't it was only a matter of time.

'An ego.'

'What?' she asked, confused.

'Your sister appears to think that she is irresistible to men.'

It was news to Rose that she wasn't.

'You, on the other hand…' He shook his head slowly, his voice fading as he continued to study her face with an intensity that bordered on compulsion.

Slowly a smile so incredibly tender that it made her heart skip several beats spread across his face, softening the hard contours and bringing a glowing warmth Rose had never seen before to the mirrored surface of his spectacular eyes.

'What about me?' she whispered. It could do no harm to listen if she didn't lose sight of the fact none of this was true. Mathieu's objective was laying claim to his child and making sure history did not repeat itself.

'You, *mon coeur*,' he observed with a husky catch in his voice, 'appear not to have the faintest idea of the effect you have on men.'

It wasn't the effect she had on men that Rose was concerned about—just one man. As her eyes lingered with a mixture of fascination and longing on the familiar stark purity of a face that would have made a sculptor's fingers tingle a tiny sigh bubbled past her clenched teeth—he was nothing less than beautiful. The sort of beauty that made a person's heart ache.

Her hand went to her stomach. Would their baby inherit his stunning looks?

'Look, you don't have to say these things.' She actually didn't need to be reminded of what she was missing. 'I'm fine with the fact that Rebecca is the sexy one and, for the record and just to save time, energy and your inventive powers, I wouldn't dream of trying to cut you out of the baby's life.'

The corners of his mouth lifted in a smile that left his grey eyes hard. 'I'd like to see you try.'

Rose flung up her hands and, grabbing hold of the billowing skirt of her gown, stood up. 'Oh, for pity's sake, I try to be nice. Offer you an olive branch and what do I get? Bloody-minded macho belligerence. Why does everything always have to be a fight with you?' she asked wearily.

'You expect me not to challenge you when you say stupid things?'

'I mean it,' she protested as he dragged a frustrated hand through his hair. 'I'm not trying to cut you out. You can be as much a part of—'

'Who told you that Rebecca is the sexy one?'

'I thought you were here because of the baby. You seem more interested in Rebecca.'

'I am here because of the baby…but mostly I'm here because I can't…' He stopped dead and searched her face. 'My God, you're jealous.'

'It's your fault,' she wailed. 'I never have been jealous of Rebecca before and, God knows, I've had enough cause. I've been fine with it, her being the sexy one.'

'You're talking rubbish and you know it.'

Rose's jaw tightened. 'What would you know? You're not a twin. You think because we're identical, give or take the odd fifteen pounds, that if one is sexy so is the other. Sexiness isn't just about looks…though it doesn't do any harm if you are a size eight.' In another century her curves might have given her the edge, but not in an era when you were judged on the smallness of your jean size.

He heard her out but his impatience was obvious. 'Have you finished? Is this the end of the lecture? You think I don't know these things are more than skin-deep?'

Rose swallowed. She had asked for honesty so it wasn't really logical to feel hurt when she got it.

'I'm sure your sister is a perfectly nice woman, but even if she put on enough flesh to lose that androgynous look the entire mood of my day would not be changed for the better by hearing her voice.'

Rose's jaw dropped. 'But Rebecca has the perfect figure.'

'No,' he contradicted firmly, 'you have the perfect figure.' His lips lifted into a smile of satisfaction as his eyes slid over her voluptuous curves. 'But we have a good deal of time to address your body issues.'

'I don't have body issues.' Her protest was automatic but not firm as she read the need in his taut expression. 'I'm just realistic.' If only that were true, she thought sombrely. She only had to catch a glimpse of him looking like all her romantic fantasies made flesh, and pretty perfect flesh too, and realism and practicality flew out the window.

He gave an expressive and very Gallic shrug. 'What reason would I have to lie, Rose? You have already said you will give me what you think I am here to claim.'

'Are you're saying you're *not* here because of the baby?' She was unable to keep the quavering note of hurt out of her voice as she added, 'If that were so, Mathieu, why did you wait ten weeks?' Ten weeks when she had waited and hoped, then finally faced reality. He wasn't coming.

'The baby is part of the reason I came, certainly,' he agreed quietly. 'But not the whole.' He passed a hand across his eyes and sighed, knowing too well how it looked. 'And I had every intention of following you the very next day, but…'

Her face stiffened as his eyes slid from hers. Clearly he couldn't look her in the eyes when he lied. 'Something else came up?' she suggested.

'In a manner of speaking, yes, it did. About eight years ago I had an accident.' His head lifted and he smiled bleakly. 'An occupational hazard.'

Rose did not smile back. The idea of Mathieu risking his life on a race track was not one that made her feel like smiling. It made her sensitive stomach muscles clench.

'I came out of it fairly unscathed. Abrasions, a few cracked ribs and—' he gestured vaguely towards his back '—a compression fracture of my thoracic spine.' He saw her eyes fly wide in alarm and added quickly, 'It was asymptomatic, no treatment required, it healed, was considered stable, and that was that.'

Rose, her heart thudding with dread, swallowed. 'And something changed?'

'I had some pain.' A man expected pain when he had slammed his fist repeatedly into a stone wall to vent his frustration because he'd let the woman he loved leave without a fight. 'I didn't think much of it, then, when I was on the helicopter the next day following you—'

'You followed me?' she said wonderingly.

'I'm stupid enough to let you go, but not *that* stupid. Of course I followed you, *mon coeur*. Only problem was by the time I reached Athens I had a slight numbness in my hand.'

She watched, horror spreading over her like an invisible freezing veil as he flexed his right hand.

'It actually got worse, quite quickly.' Nothing in his tone hinted at the terror and revulsion he had felt when the healthy body he took for granted had failed him and he had been forced to recognise the possibility it would remain that way. 'It turned out that the fracture had moved and was compressing some nerves.'

When he had told the doctors he couldn't have surgery yet because he had things to do they had informed him bluntly that delay could result in the damage being permanent.

'The best surgeon and rehabilitation was in New York, and I'm a Demetrios,' he reminded her with a self-disparaging grin. 'We always have the best.'

'You were in hospital?' How could he sound so casual? Rose felt emotionally numb as she struggled to get her head around what he was saying. As she stared she began to notice for the first time details that she had missed in the initial shock of seeing him.

Mathieu had always come across as a man with limitless reserves of energy; his dynamism was one of the things she had first noticed about him. Once she had moved beyond the sinfully sexy body and fallen angel face. The vitality he projected was almost combustible and if asked before that moment she would have confidently predicted that his reserves were limitless.

Looking at him now suggested her confidence had been misplaced; if he had been anyone else she would have said he was surviving on caffeine and adrenaline.

Normally immaculately groomed, he looked as if he hadn't shaved in a couple of days and there were crescent-moon-shaped shadows she had never seen before under his deep-set eyes that emphasised their extraordinary colour and made them look, if it were possible, even more striking

The strong, elegantly sculpted bones of his narrow oval face had acquired a sharper edge, giving his cheekbones a knifelike prominence. Her concern grew as she saw that the skin stretched over the dramatic dips and hollows had a greyish tinge normally associated with extreme exhaustion and stress or illness.

He'd been ill, seriously ill, and she hadn't been there for him.

'For a while,' he agreed, nodding. 'I was honoured Andreos came to visit, though he spent most of the time telling me that it is my fault that Sacha has accepted a place at the Sorbonne because I broke her heart.' At least one thing he had done had gone according to plan.

She hardly heard him, her head was buzzing. 'You were in hospital and I didn't know? You didn't tell me?' Her voice rose a shrill decibel with each disbelieving addition before falling to a husky sob as she added, 'And you have the nerve to say I mean something to you.'

'Tell you?' He pushed a hand through his dark hair. 'How could I tell you? So the guy does the operation a dozen times a week, it's a walk in the park for him. There was still no guarantee it would work, I could have been left a cripple.' His lean face spasmed as his molten-silver gaze raked her face. 'How could I ask you to take me like that, Rose?'

'How can you say that? I wouldn't…how can you think for a second it would make any difference to how I feel?' she protested furiously.

His chin lifted. 'I did not want your pity.'

Rose snorted. 'Pity,' she echoed. 'I could kill you for doing that alone.' A deep sob suddenly welled up from deep inside her and emerged as a shocking whimper of distress. 'How could you think it would matter to me, Mathieu?'

'It would matter to me. I want to be a whole man for you.' With a groan Mathieu took her face between his hands. 'Please don't cry,' he begged. 'Smile. I've been dreaming about your smile all these weeks. A day that passes not seeing you smile makes me feel cheated, Rose.'

Her cheeks wet with tears, her heart so full she could hardly breathe Rose reached out blindly to steady herself before she found support. His warm fingers closed over hers and she found her hand placed and held firm against his chest.

Outside the door there was the noise of a bleeper shrilling and the sound of running feet, but the din did not register with Rose. 'You like my smile?'

'Like is not quite the right word...'

She swallowed, still not quite daring to believe what she was seeing stamped into those sternly beautiful features, but wanting more than anything to allow herself to.

'I used to think my life was stimulating and productive.' A fleeting self-derisive smile tugged at the corners of his lips as he contemplated his naïvety. 'I used to think that needing someone was a weakness, now I realise that the reverse is true. It requires strength, and also admittedly a little insanity, to care for someone, to put into their hands the power to hurt or heal.' While he spoke he took Rose's hand in his and unfurled each finger like the petals of a flower. 'Such a pretty hand too,' he murmured, lifting her hand to his mouth and brushing her palm with his lips, all the time holding her eyes with his.

Rose's eyes filled with emotional tears as she blinked up at him. 'Needing someone...*me*...?'

'You are infuriating and ridiculously stubborn and also totally adorable. I have known I loved you almost from the start. I was just too afraid to admit it to myself.'

Mathieu was saying things she had never expected to hear him say outside her dreams, but she felt strangely dispassionate. Her clinical detachment wavered under the hungry, searching scrutiny of his narrowed eyes.

'You are still wary of my motives.'

'I don't want to be,' she admitted.

He ran a finger down the furrow between her feathery brows and nodded. 'Before I met you I was arrogant enough to imagine that a man had a choice about who he loved.'

'So you love me against your better judgement?' More than you expected, Rose, she reminded herself, but not enough even had she been inclined to take what he said at face value. 'Because I don't fit into your life.'

The conclusion drew a strange laugh from him. He shook his head and drew his hand heavily across his stubble-covered jaw. 'You *are* my life. Surely you know this?'

His incredulous eyes swept across her face.

'You have to know this, Rose.'

'I have to know…' she echoed, giving an odd little laugh. 'I don't think I know anything any more except that you look terrible,' she husked. 'I know you don't want my advice, but shouldn't you still be in hospital?'

'You have no idea what I want,' he retorted, covering her hand with his.

'I know you didn't want me to be a virgin.'

'*Dieu*, I know I acted like a total fool,' he groaned, lifting her hand to his lips. 'You don't know how often I wished I had not said the things I did.

'I was totally irrational, but you have no idea what a shock it was to discover…' Visibly shaken by the memory, he closed his eyes, his fingers tightening around Rose's until she winced and, mumbling an apology, he let them go.

'The truth is, Rose, that I had been rationalising my feelings for you, telling myself that it was just physical and you felt the same way, then when I discovered what a precious gift you had given me the pretence was ripped away and I had to face the reality of my feelings for you.'

Rose's heart lurched. There was no mistaking the sincerity glowing in his luminous eyes. 'Keep talking, Mathieu,' she encouraged.

'I love you, Rose...marry me...' Mathieu said, watching her face.

With a cry she was in his arms and he was holding her and kissing her with a tenderness and passion that drove her last lingering doubts away.

'You know,' she said when they broke apart, 'it's going to take a lot of those...' her eyes darkened as she followed the sensual curve of his mouth with a finger '...an awful lot,' she warned him huskily, 'to drive away the memory of these last weeks.'

His smoky gaze slid over her face. 'I will do my best,' he promised, taking her hand and, before she realised his intention, sliding the big emerald back in place. 'Now that,' he said with satisfaction, 'is where it belongs.'

'And where do I belong?'

'You have to ask? In my arms, of course.' As he pulled her to him she gave a sudden laugh.

'I've just thought—what will your father say when he finds out we're back together?'

'Does it matter? And, besides, miles may have separated us, but you were never for a moment out of my heart or thoughts.'

Enchanted by this romantic confession, she wound her arms around his neck and froze, her anxious eyes seeking his. 'The operation...I don't want to hurt you...'

'I have a scar, which I will show you later,' he promised with a look that made the heat bloom in her cheeks. 'But,' he added firmly, 'I am not fragile or breakable. I will cause metal detectors in airports some stress...' he shrugged '...but the surgery was a total success.'

Rose sighed as she felt the last cloud vanish from her emotional horizon. She struggled to stay sensible and focused even though his lips were tantalisingly close. 'About your father, though, Mat—'

His mouth a few inches from hers, Mathieu groaned.

'I really didn't mean to make things worse between you with the things I said to him.'

'My father and I are fine—well, for us fine at least.'

'Seriously?'

He nodded. 'I'll tell you about it later.' With a wave of his hand he brushed aside the subject. 'But not now.' Now there were other things he needed to tell her. He curved his hand around her face. 'You know, for a split second when Rebecca walked in through the door I thought it was you.' The joy he had felt had sprung from the depths of his soul. The bitter disappointment and sense of loss when he had realised his error had been equally profound. 'Then I saw it wasn't and it was like having heaven snatched away. I am incomplete without you, Rose.'

Rose covered her mouth with her hand as tears sprang to her eyes. 'Please don't say that if you don't mean it, Mathieu.'

'I have never meant anything more in my life.' There was no mistaking the total sincerity ringing in his statement. 'In my life I have loved people…' His eyes slid from hers as he said huskily, 'My mother…'

She watched the muscles in his brown throat work as he swallowed, clearly fighting to contain strong emotions. Heart aching with empathy, she reached out and caught his hand.

As he raised her hand to his lips his eyes lifted and connected with her wide-eyed, sympathetic gaze. His eyes not leaving hers for a moment, he opened her fingers one by one and pressed his lips to her palm. The tenderness in his expression and the gesture made her throat constrict with emotion.

When he lowered her hand he didn't release it, but kept it tightly enfolded between his big hands.

'You remind me of her sometimes.'

'I do?'

He nodded, one corner of his mouth lifting in a lopsided smile that squeezed her heart. 'Not in looks. She was very dark.' His eyes brushed her fair hair, letting the silky strands fall through his fingers. 'But she was a fighter like you and stubborn too. And her pride sometimes…' he reflected, a shadow crossing his face '…made her suffer more than was necessary, but she was never bitter, you know, or angry. I had enough anger for us both,' he admitted, dragging a hand through his dark hair.

'What I am trying to say is, Rose, that I have loved people…my mother, then my stepmother and my brother. I lost them all.

'It hurt so much that I think to avoid ever feeling that way again I sealed away my emotions and nailed down the lid.' His brooding gaze rested on her face and the grimness lifted. 'Then you came along and I no longer had any control over my feelings…' Unable to resist the temptation of her lush lips another second, he closed his mouth over hers with a hunger that drove the breath from Rose's body.

When they broke apart Rose's head was spinning and she was smiling with dreamy content.

'What I felt for you, *ma petite*, could never be confined within any box. Somehow, I knew that to lose you,' he rasped in a voice that throbbed with raw emotion, 'would be unbearable, and it was.' Eyes bleak, he drew a hand across his face as if to extinguish the memory of the last ten weeks. 'For delivering me from my private hell a day early, I will always be grateful to your sister.'

'Me too,' Rose admitted. 'I can't imagine what your father made of her.'

'He did mention the fact that it could be worse—she might be the one I had to marry.'

'*Had* to marry? Nice to know he approves,' she teased, running a loving hand down his lean cheek.

'Approves might be a little strong,' he admitted, turning his face into her hand and pressing a warm kiss into the small palm.

When accused of turning his back on his parental responsibilities, Mathieu—already shaken to the core by the news he was about to be a father—had retorted without his usual self-restraint that this comment was nothing short of breathtaking hypocrisy.

In the following bitter exchange the simmering resentment of years had spilled out. Even that eavesdropped conversation from years before had been dredged up and in his turn Andreos had accused Mathieu of being a thankless wretch incapable of showing affection and always looking for an opportunity to throw his generosity back in his face.

In the end Mathieu had turned his back with every intention of walking away for good, and he would have except he had happened to look back to deliver one final comment.

It was a comment that he had never voiced, nor had he walked out of the door. Andreos Demetrios, the man who could make other strong men wilt with a look, had been standing, his face contorted with grief, as tears ran unchecked down his cheeks.

Mathieu had only paused for a moment before he had moved to comfort him. He had listened while his father had told him that if he had stayed outside that door a little longer he would have heard the rest of the conversation.

A conversation in which Andreos had admitted to his wife that he knew it was irrational to blame a child for his own sins, even if it was guilt that made him unable to show affection to his older son—that and the belief that the boy hated him.

It would have been an overstatement to say that the past had been washed away, but it was a beginning, which was just as well because he suspected that Rose would not rest until she had seen everyone kiss and make up.

'So you're marrying me because your father tells you to...?' She laughed.

His eyes darkened as he caught her passionately to him and growled, 'I'm marrying you because I adore every hair on your glorious head. I've just made a very interesting discovery.'

'You have?' she asked, letting her head fall back as he kissed the base of her throat.

'There is no back in this thing.' He laid his hand on the smooth curve of her bottom that was exposed to the elements and the gaze of anyone who happened to look through the glass panel in the door.

With a shriek of protest Rose backed away, holding the sides of her gaping gown together. 'Stay away from me. This is a hospital and the radiologist could come back any moment.' Conscious this was a very real possibility, Rose retook her place on the couch and rearranged the blanket primly over her legs. 'You,' she warned, 'keep your distance.'

Mathieu looked at her, a wicked glint glittering in his eyes. 'You don't get turned on by the idea of being caught in the act, then?' He watched her blush... *Dieu*, but he loved that blush.

'No, I do not...' She slid him a curious look. 'Do you?'

Mathieu threw back his head and roared with laughter. 'Oh, I'm dark and twisted—ask anyone.'

'I like to form my own opinion,' she told him, dimpling prettily.

He folded his arms across his chest and strolled over to her side. 'And what's your opinion of me?'

He recognised the irony. He'd spent his entire adult life not giving a damn what anyone thought of him and now there was someone who he desperately wanted to think well of him. The most surprising thing was recognising the new vulnerability did not appall him as it once might.

'Too soon to tell. Ask me again in twenty years or so.'

'I will,' he promised thickly.

Rose's eyes filled as he laid a warm hand over her abdomen. 'This baby, *mon coeur*, you're happy about it...?'

'More,' she promised with a palpable sincerity that drove the last trace of lingering uncertainty from his face, 'than you can imagine.'

'So tell me,' he said, dragging a chair and placing it beside her. 'About this scan? Is the image 3D? Do we get a DVD? Are—?'

She held up her hand, laughing. 'Oh, no, you're going to be one of those men who cut the cord, aren't you?'

'Hell, no,' he drawled, giving a visible shudder. 'I'll stick to moral support.' He caught her small hand to his lips. 'It is my job to keep you safe, *ma petite*, and I will,' he swore solemnly, 'do that with the last breath in my body. I will do that.'

'Oh, Mathieu.'

The radiologist returned a few minutes later. She paused, shocked, on the threshold for a moment before silently retracing her steps.

She waited a tactful space of time before returning, making sure that a tone-deaf wall could have heard her approach.

The pink-cheeked and tousle-haired mother-to-be with the just-kissed look smiled as she walked in and said brightly, 'We were just wondering what had happened to you.'

Her partner grinned. 'That was not what you said you were wondering about to me, *mon ange*.'

The technician cast him a reproachful look, but thawed towards him when she saw the tears in his eyes as he looked at the first images of his unborn child.

A man who looked like him, and he was in touch with his emotions—now that, in her experience, was rare. But not perhaps as rare as the look the couple exchanged as they linked hands.

'We did this?' Mathieu breathed as he stared with sparkling eyes at the tiny image magnified on the screen. 'You are brilliant!'

Rose smiled at his enthusiasm and awe. 'I can't take all the credit. This was a joint effort.'

'We're a team.'

Rose gave a sigh of content. 'Totally,' she agreed, seeing no limits to what they could achieve together. She was the luckiest woman alive.

MILLS & BOON

MODERN™

On sale 4th January 2008

THE ITALIAN BILLIONAIRE'S RUTHLESS REVENGE
by Jacqueline Baird

Guido Barberi's ex-wife left him – along with a quarter of
a million pounds! Now he'll have his revenge... Can Sara
resist his skilful campaign to seduce her into his bed...?

ACCIDENTALLY PREGNANT, CONVENIENTLY WED
by Sharon Kendrick

Aisling's frumpy suits meant Gianluca Palladio had never
given her a second look. Then Gianluca glimpses the real
woman beneath... Suddenly Aisling and Gianluca are
bound together forever...by a baby!

THE SHEIKH'S CHOSEN QUEEN
by Jane Porter

Jesslyn has been summoned to the desert land that
Sheikh Sharif rules. Jesslyn refuses to take orders, but Sharif
is determined: she will obey his ultimate command and
submit – to becoming his wife and queen!

THE FRENCHMAN'S MARRIAGE DEMAND
by Chantelle Shaw

Billionaire Zac Deverell is angry that Freya is claiming
her baby as his – he has reasons to be sure he's not
the father. But one thing *is* for certain – if the baby is
his, he'll take Freya as his wife...

Available at WHSmith, Tesco, ASDA, and all good bookshops
www.millsandboon.co.uk

1207/01b

MILLS & BOON
MODERN
On sale 4th January 2008

THE MILLIONAIRE'S CONVENIENT BRIDE
by Catherine George

Connah Carey Jones needs a temporary housekeeper and
nanny for his young daughter and Hester Ward is perfect.
Soon Connah proposes their business arrangement include
marriage... But is Hester prepared to be just a convenient wife?

EXPECTING HIS LOVE-CHILD
by Carol Marinelli

Brooding billionaire Levander Kolovsky doesn't want a
permanent woman in his life, or an heir. But ordinary girl
Millie has returned to share her secret: she's expecting
Levander's baby...

THE GREEK TYCOON'S UNEXPECTED WIFE
by Annie West

Stavros Denakis is furious when Tessa Marlowe turns up
without warning. Cynical through his experience with women,
Stavros suspects the wife he hardly knows is a gold-digger.
But Tessa is a temptation he can't resist...

THE ITALIAN'S CAPTIVE VIRGIN
by India Grey

Tycoon Angelo Emiliani wants to buy Anna Delafield's French
château, but she'll do anything to stop him. So he decides
to teach her a lesson! Soon Anna's at risk of losing her
virginity and more...!

Available at WHSmith, Tesco, ASDA, and all good bookshops
www.millsandboon.co.uk

1207/06

MILLS & BOON

MODERN Heat

On sale 4th January 2008

LAYING DOWN THE LAW
by Susan Stephens

Sheltered and naïve Carly Tate is out of her depth.
Dark, dangerous Lorenzo Domenico isn't only her mentor
and tutor, he's also the first man to make her heart race.
But she knows the gorgeous Italian will never see past her
frumpy clothes and embarrassing innocence. Little does she
realise that, to Lorenzo, Carly is a breath of fresh air...

HIS MISTRESS, HIS TERMS
by Trish Wylie

Rich, gorgeous playboy Alex Fitzgerald has his sights
set on Merrow O'Connell. Initially he needs her interior
design skills, but soon they're on different terms – she's
perfect mistress material! Merrow has learned not to let
anyone close and is determined to stay single – so what
will she do when the billionaire playboy wants her to
be *more* than just his mistress...?

Available at WHSmith, Tesco, ASDA, and all good bookshops
www.millsandboon.co.uk

100 Reasons to Celebrate

2008 is a very special year as we celebrate Mills and Boon's Centenary.

Each month throughout the year there will be something new and exciting to mark the centenary, so watch for your favourite authors, captivating new stories, special limited edition collections…and more!

www.millsandboon.co.uk

4 Books
and a surprise gift!

We would like to take this opportunity to thank you for reading this Mills & Boon® book by offering you the chance to take FOUR more specially selected titles from the Modern™ series absolutely FREE! We're also making this offer to introduce you to the benefits of the Mills & Boon® Reader Service™—

- ★ **FREE home delivery**
- ★ **FREE gifts and competitions**
- ★ **FREE monthly Newsletter**
- ★ **Exclusive Reader Service offers**
- ★ **Books available before they're in the shops**

Accepting these FREE books and gift places you under no obligation to buy, you may cancel at any time, even after receiving your free shipment. Simply complete your details below and return the entire page to the address below. You don't even need a stamp!

YES! Please send me 4 free Modern books and a surprise gift. I understand that unless you hear from me, I will receive 6 superb new titles every month for just £2.89 each, postage and packing free. I am under no obligation to purchase any books and may cancel my subscription at any time. The free books and gift will be mine to keep in any case.

P7ZEF

Ms/Mrs/Miss/Mr .... Initials ....

Surname .... **BLOCK CAPITALS PLEASE**

Address ....

....

.... Postcode ....

Send this whole page to:
UK: FREEPOST CN81, Croydon, CR9 3WZ

Offer valid in UK only and is not available to current Mills & Boon® Reader Service™ subscribers to this series. Overseas and Eire please write for details. We reserve the right to refuse an application and applicants must be aged 18 years or over. Only one application per household. Terms and prices subject to change without notice. Offer expires 28th February 2008. As a result of this application, you may receive offers from Harlequin Mills & Boon and other carefully selected companies. If you would prefer not to share in this opportunity please write to The Data Manager, PO Box 676, Richmond, TW9 1WU.

Mills & Boon® is a registered trademark owned by Harlequin Mills & Boon Limited.
Modern™ is being used as a trademark. The Mills & Boon® Reader Service™ is being used as a trademark.